Dear Reader,

I knew from the first that since I was an immigrant steelworker's son, I wasn't a suitable mate for a high-society, Pittsburgh girl like Abigail Bainbridge.

But I as conceited enough to think rules like that weren't made for a guy like me.

So I loved her anyway—with disastrous consequences.

Eight terrible years passed, but I could neither forget nor forgive. So, when Abbie stood at the altar about to marry the wimpy paragon of her mother's fondest dreams—what half-crazed, vengeance-seeking idiot should show up at the church in jeans and muddy boots and scream the bride's name? Whose possessive arms did Abbie rush into? Who did she run away with?

You guessed it, the wrong man—me.

I thought all I wanted was revenge, until Abbie loved me even more tenderly than before. Then I found out that Abbie had kept the most terrible kind of secret. But not even that could part us for long. Because I'd learned the hard way that the reason I'd never forgotten her had nothing to do with revenge and everything to do with love.

Grant Nichols

ANN MAJOR

Ann major lives in Texas with her husband of many years, and is the mother of three grown children. She has a master's degree from Texas A&M at Kingsville, Texas, and is a former English teacher. She is a founding board member of the RWA and a frequent speaker at writers' groups.

Ann loves to write; she considers her ability to do so a gift. Her hobbies include hiking in the mountains, sailing, ocean kayaking, traveling and playing the piano. But most of all she enjoys her family.

Ann Major
The Wrong Man

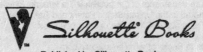

Published by Silhouette Books
America's Publisher of Contemporary Romance

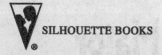

SILHOUETTE BOOKS

ISBN-13: 978-0-373-36041-3
ISBN-10:   0-373-36041-X

THE WRONG MAN

Copyright © 1984 by Ann Major

Published Silhouette Books 1984, 1993

One

Abigail Bainbridge tore her eyes from the mirror, from the terrifying vision of herself in white satin and lace, and ran trembling toward the window. Her rough and tumble movements caused the gauzy veil to snag on the leg of an antique mauve-velvet chair. In her impatience she kicked the chair aside, momentarily forgetting that in this house antiques were as sacred as cows in India. She contemplated the object of her sacrilege with only the faintest twinge of remorse. After all, what was it really but just an old, faded chair, and a very old chair at that? It creaked and wobbled so much, she was afraid to sit in it. Then in an equally unladylike frenzy of pin-pulling and tulle-tearing, Abigail yanked the veil back into place.

The tulle ripped. This brought more than a twinge of remorse, as she recalled the extravagant price of her gown. What was the matter with her? This morning she was not cool and poised, as she generally strived so hard to be. Her intensely blue eyes flashed with unusual violence, though her face was white and still. She felt damnably cross and put upon. Even her thinking was askew. Ladies didn't think emotionally and use coarse language. Abigail Bainbridge was a lady of position in the world, and she needed to think and act like one. Her mother had carefully taught her that, though for years Abigail had stubbornly resisted the education.

It had seemed so dreary—behaving properly at all times. Do this! Don't do that! There were rules for everything, and it was difficult to remember them all. Abigail had always wondered why she couldn't just be herself. In *this* house a child couldn't pick up a fork and jab it into a carrot or potato without a lecture. No, one had to pick up the right fork with the right hand and hold it in the right way. But the fork rules weren't of the sort that had bothered her the most.

The rules about people were the killers. People were just like forks really—the right ones to know, the right ones to love, the right ways to behave toward them. The only difference was that the lectures involving people were longer and more complicated and much more upsetting.

These things had been impossible for her to understand when she was young. Even after she had accepted that the Bainbridge way really was the only way one could live and have things go decently, it had been terribly difficult for her. Sometimes she still felt so stifled she wanted to scream and pound the wall and do all sorts of things Bainbridges never did, or at least never admitted that they did. She wanted... What did she want? She wished that life were different—her life at least.

To the world she presented herself as a carefully composed woman who didn't go in for such savageries as wall-pounding and chair-kicking, a young woman dedicated to the same lofty pursuits as generations of noble Bainbridges before her. But no matter how hard she tried, she couldn't be this paragon full-time as her mother was. There had been embarrassing lapses even in public—though thankfully not since quite some time.

Abigail could escape from the responsibilities of her station in life only when she was in her apartment or studio and completely alone. Then she allowed herself to give in to the wild, disordered side of her nature that had once almost destroyed her. She kept her studio as messy as a child's playroom, and kept herself that way, too, slopping around in paint-spattered jeans and T-shirts, glorying in her niche of freedom. She excused this one escape from her assigned station in life as the need of an artist to have at least a modicum of mental freedom.

Abigail stared out the window. Through the security bars she could see her seven-year-old son, Michael, playing in the litter of fall leaves that the gardener was carefully raking into piles. The bars on the window made her feel like a prisoner. She stared down at her child, who was running to and fro on the carpet of autumn gold.

She had a strange impulse to throw open the window and call down to her son so that he would look up and wave to her, to the woman he called Auntie Abigail. Michael did not know that she was his natural mother. Only her parents and she herself knew this galling truth, and it was one of the most carefully guarded secrets in all of Pittsburgh society, the proverbial skeleton locked safely away in one of the many ample closets of her mother's prestigious mansion.

And, oh Lord, thank heavens for those closets, for Bainbridges and Harrisons had no room in their well-ordered world for clandestine affairs and illegitimate babies! Were Harold Harrison to discover the blemished state of his bride-to-be's past, he would surely turn that ugly, mottled red that made every freckle bristle as brightly as a ripe raspberry ready to be picked, and Abigail wouldn't have blamed him. Not even youth and a passionately wild nature not yet carefully curbed could excuse such gross mistakes, even eight years later.

The window Abigail stood before, like every window in her mother's house, was locked and tightly sealed. Again Abigail felt imprisoned, and she dug her fingers into the thick coil of damask drapes. Once more she wondered what was the matter with her. Why was she so nervous? There was no danger of Harold discovering the truth, and she didn't feel guilty about concealing it from him. She knew that she was no longer the same wild rebel she'd been. She'd atoned for what she'd done long ago. She would be a good wife to Harold. Then, what was her problem? The cool, reserved Bainbridge training had taught her little patience with the emotional upheaval she was experiencing.

Abigail had scarcely recognized herself a moment before. The bright-eyed, chalky face in the mirror had been that of a woman in desperate trouble, not that of a cool sophisticated young woman with her life firmly in control. Nor did she look the radiant bride very much in love with Harold, as the newspapers exuded after every elaborate society fete held in her honor.

When she thought of her dear, ever-so-proper

Harold, a wan smile played fleetingly along her sensual mouth. Of course, she was in love with him, very much so. He was exactly what she needed. When she was with him, it wasn't so difficult to suppress the troublesome side of her personality.

But if this was what she wanted, why did she feel so strange and so terribly unhappy? It wasn't as if she'd rushed into anything. She and Harold had been engaged for over a year. He'd been too considerate to rush her.

The wedding was to take place in two weeks. Wasn't it a little premature for bridal jitters?

Abigail stared down at her son as he played. At least when she married she could claim him as her own. He could live with her at last, and she could be the mother to him she'd always dreamed of being. Before she'd met Harold, she'd begged her mother to grant her custody of her son without the price of marriage. But Rosalind had said she would never do that. Once—before Harold started courting her—Abigail had felt so desperate she'd considered marriage just to have Michael as her own.

Abigail balled one hand into a clenched knot of flesh and bone and pounded against the window, hoping that Michael would look up and see her. But he didn't. He went on playing, unaware of the woman in the second story window.

Everything had worked out so perfectly. She

would have Michael and Harold, and Rosalind, her mother, would be happy with this oh-so-suitable marriage.

Suitable. The word echoed uneasily in Abigail's mind. In the more rebellious days of her youth, Abigail had hated that word because it was her mother's favorite. It symbolized all the Bainbridge rules of right and wrong, the blacks and whites of their carefully controlled world.

Her pulse was pounding violently in her throat. A dark and terrible emotion possessed her. She felt doomed, and she didn't know why.

In agitation she pushed back a strand of the thick tumble of dark gold hair that framed the delicate oval of her face. Her hair, beautiful and thick, was the color of the rich autumn leaves fluttering outside in the light October breeze. Normally she restrained it in a knot at the nape of her neck, but for some unaccountable reason, she hadn't felt like wearing it that way today. Instead she was wearing it as Grant had loved it all those years ago, falling loosely about her shoulders.

Grant! Even his name could still numb every feeling she had. With all the stubborn control she could muster, she pushed him from her mind. Even so, the mere thought of him had left her whole body trembling.

It was the wedding gown and what it symbolized

that upset her! She'd put it on because her mother wanted to approve her appearance. The finality of what was going to happen in fourteen days was striking her.

She was making a commitment to a man a second time, and even though Harold was a man of principles, a man who accepted the profound responsibilities of his position in life, and even though he followed the same sacred rules she'd been taught to live by herself, she was afraid. She had no fear of standing at his side as hostess at affairs that were so grand most women would have quaked with nerves at the thought. She could converse easily with the rich and famous of Harold's world; she had been groomed all her life for just such an illustrious marriage. Her worry was simply a reflection that once before she'd made a commitment to a man and seen her life blow up in her face. Of course, that had been long ago when she was young and foolish and had rebelled against the vast honor of having been born a Bainbridge. She'd forgotten her place and made the terrible mistake of choosing the wrong man.

It was an error she'd determined never to make again. She was graciously charming to everyone, the perfect lady her mother had taught her to be. But when men responded to her charm, she froze them with the most quelling reserve. Having known passion eight years before and suffered from its consequences, she distrusted all man-woman relationships. Since her seventeenth summer, she'd never again been able to respond to any man's touch, not even Harold's.

She'd gone on with her life. Her parents had always tried to pretend it hadn't happened, and she'd tried to follow their stoic example. She hadn't wanted to explore her disturbing feelings, her curious emptiness toward men. Bainbridges believed painful emotions were private and best shut inside oneself, where they were less troublesome. They had no use for such modern absurdities as psychiatry and therapy. One had duties and goals and responsibilities; it was selfish to dwell on one's own needs.

She had gone on living, but she was a beautiful shell. The vibrant, wild creature who had once lived inside her had fled. She did all the correct and proper things that were expected of her, and the few men she had dated had inevitably grown bored with the imperturbable nonpareil she was—all except Harold.

Thankfully, Harold hadn't expected passion. He was satisfied with a wife who was docile and beautiful—and a member of one of the oldest and wealthiest industrial families in Pittsburgh. She was the kind of wife he was expected to marry, just as he was the kind of husband expected of her. It was, as her mother Rosalind said approvingly, ''so very suitable.''

Eight years ago Rosalind had thought Grant, the son of a common steelworker and the man Abigail had loved "so very unsuitable!"

Though Abigail rarely allowed herself to think of him, Grant was not the hazily remembered dream she pretended he was. If only he were! The remnants of a snapshot she'd taken of him lay hidden in one of her dresser drawers just as the secret, forbidden treasure of his love lay buried in her heart.

Long ago, desperately savage with grief, she'd ripped up the picture. Then, realizing it was the only picture she had to remember him by, she'd carefully collected all the pieces and pasted them back together again. But she didn't need that crudely pasted, tearstained picture. She could see him as clearly in her mind's eye as she'd seen him the first summer afternoon she'd met him in the hilly woods of central Pennsylvania all those years ago.

Away from Rosalind and the well-ordered Bainbridge world, Abigail had felt as gloriously free and untamed as the primitive forest. She'd been fishing in the creek that bordered her Aunt Peggy's vast estate and was walking proudly home with a rather nice catch slung over her shoulder when she discovered that she'd somehow taken the wrong path and gotten lost.

Suddenly she'd heard a girl's low laughter mingle seductively with the husky music of a man's voice.

Stepping into a clearing, she'd seen a small cottage dwarfed beneath enormous trees. A man who was tall, well over six feet, was casually leaning his great muscular frame down against the door of a flashy white convertible in which sat a matching pair of flashy black-haired beauties, fitting companions for a man with his dark good looks. His air was that of amused, brotherly indulgence as he chatted with the two girls, who were shamelessly competing for his attention.

Then suddenly he'd looked up, and if Abigail lived ten decades, she would never forget the intensity of his handsome face in that thrilling moment. The warm boldness of his gaze swept her in what she guessed was the usual insolent visual caress he tossed all women when first he saw them. It was a look of frankly male appraisal. She'd flushed and had suddenly found it impossible to draw a breath. She was not used to men looking at her like that; she had been too carefully sheltered. His expression changed almost at once, as though he sensed her innocence and sought to protect it, as though even in that first moment he realized how special she would become to him.

She'd lost awareness of anything except him. The forest noises were a vague blur—the quiet sounds of maple and birch leaves rustling in the breeze, the lively chatter of birds in the overhead branches, the distant gurgle of the splashing creek. She was breathlessly aware only of him.

In those timeless few seconds she memorized every detail of his appearance. He was tall, an indolent giant of a man, lean and yet powerfully built, so different from the pampered rich boys she was used to dating. She didn't know that his aura of lean toughness, which so attracted her, had been acquired when he'd been growing up on the rough side of Pittsburgh near the steel mills.

A great untidy shock of dark auburn hair fell over his brow, glistening as though freshly washed in the streaks of sunlight sifting through the trees. His skin was so tanned she instantly thought of warm, vibrant mahogany. Beneath brows that were thick and black, his darkly lashed eyes, too, were black. Brilliant and intense, his eyes were his one truly beautiful feature. They alone softened the harshness of his face, the features so rugged they seemed carved from dark, living stone.

How she came to glory in the sensitivity of those beautiful eyes, which later so easily learned to read her soul. How she admired the rough-cut handsomeness of his masculine features. He had a full sensual mouth, and even in that first moment, though she was then too innocent to fully understand, she'd sensed he was a passionate man. The softness of his lips when exploring her flesh in days thereafter always amazed her. The only soft thing about him had been the way he touched her.

It was fitting that when she first met him he was in the company of two women. He was a man much admired by women, though he insisted his interest in them was more often brotherly than not. The baby brother of five older sisters, he'd been spoiled by women from the cradle, and he took their adoration for granted. He liked women, and they liked him.

That afternoon Abigail knew nothing of his character, and like all those other women, she was instantly drawn to him. She was naive and uncertain; knowing nothing of men, and thought him the most attractive man in all the world. It was only later that she realized she'd fallen foolishly, irrevocably in love with a total stranger the first day she met him. She was too young to suspect he had ulterior motives.

"Hey, girls," he said, tearing his gaze from Abigail and reluctantly returning his attention to the two in the car, "I told you, you'd better leave before you got me in trouble." The sheer music of his voice flowed through Abigail. The two in the car twittered in disbelief. "And now you've done it, because here's my girlfriend." Abigail could scarcely believe he meant her, but his instant grimace of mock terror was certainly directed toward her. "There's the devil to pay when the green-eyed monster bites her.'' Abigail saw that his black eyes were twinkling.

In a daze of wonder and elation, Abigail saw the girls drive away, their sporty white car vanishing down the sun-dappled road and leaving her very much alone with the compelling stranger. It was a glorious, triumphant moment. The rest of the afternoon had been a time of enchantment.

In a faltering voice she'd asked, ''Why did you tell them I was your girlfriend?''

His black eyes held hers, and it was as if she'd known him always. ''Because you are...now,'' he murmured.

She flushed with the excitement of first love and at the wonder and newness of him. She was not used to men treating her as he did.

When he'd taken her fish, offering to clean them for her, she'd let him.

''Those girls,'' she'd begun, ''I hope they didn't leave because of me.''

Of course, she really hoped that they had. She pretended to watch his knife as it flashed in swift sure strokes across the scales of the fish, but she was really watching him, admiring the bronzed color of him, the reddish highlights gleaming in his dark hair, the play of muscle in his strong arms.

''Don't give them another thought,'' he'd replied easily. ''I have five sisters, and I guess because I

was the only boy in a household of females, I had
to learn to get along with girls early in order to
survive. Anyway, ever since I can remember, girls
have been chasing me, and I've been running. Mind
you, I'm not complaining. Other guys have always
envied me." He paused, his white smile devastating
her senses. "Only today…" Again he held her gaze
intently. "…when I saw you, I stopped running."

She'd stared up at him wordlessly.

Time seemed to stand still in that breathless moment. Later she decided that was the instant she fell
in love with him. Her love deepened every time she
saw him after that. He made her feel so very special,
as though she were the only woman for him. All the
other women, who seemed to be constantly in the
background, were forgotten. The drowsy drifting
days swept away much too quickly. They were always together, and they lost themselves in the intense passion of their love. It never occurred to her
to doubt his love.

She could still remember his easy laughter, the
warm look in his beautiful eyes when she caught
him watching her. It was a picture frozen in time
and pain. He'd subsequently betrayed her and left
her to face her mother and the consequences of their
love alone.

It was easy to remember what Grant looked like
and what he was like, for her son, Michael, was his

diminutive replica. From the characteristic widow's peak and auburn hair to his quick temper, sense of humor, and attractiveness to the opposite sex, Michael was Grant's son.

It wasn't easy to forget a man, when one had to live with such a forceful reminder. Still, she knew she wouldn't have forgotten him anyway, no matter how much she might have wanted to. Most of the time, however, she never allowed herself to think of him. He had no place in her life.

She wondered suddenly if the years had changed Grant as much as they'd changed her. Had they been kind, or was he fat and old-looking and married to a plump wife with a house full of children?

A brisk hand tapped at the door, and recognizing those efficient taps instantly, Abigail composed her features into the smooth mask her mother expected, then turned dutifully toward the sound.

"Darling!" The endearment was given as a high-pitched command.

Rosalind Bainbridge swept regally into the room. "You were supposed to come down when you were dressed!"

"I'm sorry, Mother."

Rosalind's carefully arched brows rose slightly, giving her the look of a disdainful schoolteacher correcting a naughty child rather than that of the grand dame of Pittsburgh society that she was, reproving her grown daughter. Rosalind choked back a little gasp of disapproval as her critical gaze swept her daughter a second time. Then with her own taffeta dress rustling like ripping tissue paper, Rosalind rushed purposefully to her daughter's side to mend the disaster.

"Your veil's a little lopsided. I hope it doesn't do that the day of the wedding."

Abigail ignored her mother's steel-gray eyes, which pierced her with the exact intensity of her voice.

"When you were a child, it never ceased to amaze me how you used to come to pieces in a minute," Rosalind was saying, having reached Abigail's side. "I'd hardly have you dressed than you'd have your dress torn, your sash undone, and your hair in tangles."

"Like a pretty Christmas package being wildly ripped apart," Abigail said in a suddenly tender voice, remembering her father's fond words when he described the same catastrophe. He at least had understood his daughter's lusty exuberance. It had been so much more fun being a tomboy than being the beautiful, ever so proper doll her mother had wanted her to be. But eight years ago she'd lost that vibrant passion. Now she was content to be what her mother wanted.

Rosalind smiled, for her husband's apt description

of their spirited child had been a favorite of hers as well. She truly loved her daughter, and her maternal efforts to govern her child's life were based solely on a strong conviction that she was helping.

"Now...take your hands out of your hair while I pin this veil again," Rosalind directed in an unusually soft tone.

It was always like this between them when they were getting along: Rosalind commanding and Abigail silently obeying. The price of a pleasant relationship with her mother had long been total surrender.

Rosalind removed several bobby pins and placed them between her pursed lips. "I want you to wear your hair up for the wedding, and not in this...this tumble-down wild arrangement. In this state you hardly look like the suitable girl for Harold...for a Harrison," she mumbled between the pins.

"Mother, you say the name Harrison as if it were quite remarkable, akin to something saintly...or godly."

The literal-minded Rosalind entirely missed the soft irony in her daughter's remark.

"It practically is...in Pittsburgh, darling. You know that! It's so wonderful to think that you are marrying into that family."

The thought produced no elation in Abigail, only an odd sinking feeling.

Rosalind almost purred with pride. Indeed, her expression was one of intense feline satisfaction. She looked like a disdainful, plump silver cat, who after having finished a bowl of rich cream and licking the last droplet of this delicious repast from her whiskers, was ready to curl before a warm fire, content that everything of importance was right in her narrow world.

"Such a suitable match—a Harrison and a Bainbridge," Rosalind continued. "I couldn't have planned anything more eminently suitable myself. Why, you're the talk of the town! Do you know that Margaret Allison is just green with envy. She was sure her Lauren would land Harold." Rosalind smiled with smug satisfaction at the pleasant memory of Margaret's pinched features when she'd told her friend of the engagement over bridge one afternoon at the country club. "At last you'll be suitably settled. No more of your wildness."

"Mother! I haven't been wild in years!"

"I know, dear, but…I must confess I've always been a little afraid…you might…well… Anyway, I'm just glad you're marrying, that's all. Harold's just right for you. He's been such a calming influence, and as his wife, you'll become the gracious hostess I always dreamed of you being. You're going to be such an asset to him professionally. Only a Bainbridge would be suitable."

Suitable. There was that word again. An indefinable emotion flared in Abigail. It was a strange, uncomfortable feeling. For the first time in a long time she felt she needed space...time...

Mother and daughter gave one another a lengthy look of assessment. As always, Rosalind's grooming was impeccable, her expression indomitable.

Rosalind, who had once been beautiful, was still a woman of commanding presence. She dressed in beautifully coordinated outfits that flattered her matronly figure. Today she was on her way to a garden party, and she wore aqua taffeta that intensified the color of her pale gray eyes. Those eyes had a way of peering down her narrow aquiline nose with a regal look of freezing disdain when she disapproved of something, an expression that was all too familiar to Abigail. Thin, unsmiling lips were carefully outlined with just the right color of lipstick and gloss. Gleaming hair, artificially silvered, was pulled tightly into a coiled bun at the nape of her neck. Not a hair dared to be out of place. Rosalind Bainbridge had the strong features of a woman long accustomed to getting her way in all things.

Rosalind glowed with maternal pride. Abigail had always been beautiful, her outward beauty reflecting the beauty of her heart. But Rosalind knew that her daughter could never have achieved her restrained elegance and sophistication had it not been for her own influence; Abigail's true nature was too exuberant. Rosalind had fought many a battle to stamp out the wild streak that had so horrified her. Now at last, with this grand marriage an imminent reality, total victory in their lifelong war of wills was almost hers. Still, with Abigail, Rosalind could never quite rest easy. Perhaps one last word of warning might be appropriate.

"Abigail, darling, please promise me you'll try to be serious on your wedding day. None of your pranks...or accidents. And don't tease people. Getting married is a solemn occasion."

"You make it sound like a funeral, Mother." It was beginning to feel strangely like one, Abigail thought dismally.

"Darling, I was merely trying to point out that it just wouldn't be suitable if you—"

"I'm tired of being suitable and proper and elegant...and...and...everything else you're always trying to make me, Mother." Abigail lashed out passionately. "I don't even know who I am anymore! Or what I want!" She stopped herself, stunned by what she'd said.

"I can't imagine why you say that, dear," her mother returned calmly, who was accustomed to ignoring all opposition, however passionate. "You do dress nicely when you go out, but you're the last thing from elegant in your apartment—the way you

run around in that studio of yours in those awful
jeans and tight T-shirts—braless!—with a dob of
paint on your nose and your hair streaming down
your back like a wild, blond mane.'' Rosalind had
emphasized the word *braless* because she heartily
disapproved of what she considered the most horrid
fashion fad of the century. "Thank goodness you
never took Harold there!''

"I can hardly paint in designer outfits. I'm an
artist, not a fashion model!'' Abigail responded with
only faint impatience, her anger having died quickly,
as it always did. This was an old argument she practically knew by heart.

"I've never understood why you took up art. You
didn't need a career. If you simply had to have one,
you could have chosen a career that was so much
more—''

"Suitable?'' Abigail finished in a saccharine
voice.

"Exactly. Still, you could dress decently, especially now that you've become successful.''

"You mean commercial.''

"Whatever. At least you're finally getting paid,
and handsomely.''

For a fleeting instant Abigail thought of her
brightly dotted flower pictures, which were the rage
for miles around. Amazingly, they hung in the
homes of many wives of prominent men. Even Har-

old approved of them. He had hung two in his law offices.

They were lovely pictures, but they were hardly the sort of thing that inspired the respect of a professional artist. One of these days Abigail wanted to get back to serious painting. She'd only started painting the flower pictures because an interior decorator friend, Julia, had admired one she'd done for her mother on a whim after Rosalind had kept saying she wanted a flower picture that exactly matched the colors in her solarium.

Abigail had scoffed at her mother for wanting a picture to match her room. She felt that one should choose a picture because of the integrity of the painting, not because it fit a certain decor. But every one of her mother's friends had exclaimed over the picture as though it were a masterpiece, and each wanted one similar to it for her home.

It was very simple really. Pictures were like people and forks. Julia had made her see that there were many women like her mother and her friends and that if she went into custom painting for these women, painting the right pictures for the right rooms, they would sell. And because Abigail had wanted to be independent of her parents financially so that she could lead her own life without their constant interference, she'd gone into business with Julia. Together they'd built a very profitable business, but even though the money was good, Abigail had remained artistically dissatisfied.

It was only later that Abigail realized that it was Rosalind who was proud of her daughter's work and local acclaim. She felt little personal satisfaction herself. Her mother had continued to interfere in her life just as much as ever, even though money was no longer an issue.

"Ouch, Mother!" Rosalind had jabbed her scalp with a pin.

"I'm sorry, darling."

"I wish we could have a simple wedding instead of this production. You should have let me plan everything," Abigail said, thinking that maybe it was the fuss that was getting to her.

"I don't think a small wedding would have been—"

"I know...suitable."

"Besides, if I'd let you make the wedding arrangements, you'd have dreamed up something wildly impossible like getting married barefoot in the surf, you and Harold saying your own vows to each other under the stars."

Abigail giggled, her good humor momentarily restored. "I can't imagine Harold wading out into the chilly surf in rolled up trousers in October. Those ever-so-remarkable Harrison feet might get wet and gritty with sand." She paused. "Why, Mother!"

Abigail's vibrant voice rang with genuine surprise, and suddenly she was chuckling. Her blue eyes flashed with amusement. "It's amazing you even thought of that. Deep down you are a romantic! And to think in all these years I never guessed." She whirled and embraced her mother affectionately, heedless that she was crushing both their gowns. "What a marvelous idea!"

"I was afraid you'd approve," came her mother's wry retort. "I wouldn't have mentioned it at all if it wasn't too late to change our plans." Gently Rosalind disengaged herself. "Don't darling, you're wrinkling us." But the reproof lacked her former sternness, and she was smiling warmly at her lovely child. "But to answer your question, after raising someone as errant as yourself these past twenty-five years, one's mind can't help but run in some very strange channels."

It was like that between them. They loved one another deeply in spite of Rosalind's determination to run Abigail's life and Abigail's own fervent desire for independence. Her mother continued speaking affectionately, but Abigail was no longer listening. Her mother's words had stirred the embers of an old and very painful memory. She was staring out into space remembering another time and another place—that other lifetime when she had tried to be bold and independent with such devastating consequences.

It was again her seventeenth summer, three delightful, carefree months spent at Aunt Peggy's, away from her mother's harsh restrictions. Aunt Peggy had let her run as wild as the animals that lived on the vast expanse of the game preserve surrounding her estate. Her glorious love affair had started quite by accident that day she'd gone fishing, the day she'd met Grant Nichols. He was a twenty-six-year-old bachelor, house-sitting for a couple who owned the cottage in the woods that bordered Aunt Peggy's estate. He was a third-year medical student on summer break.

Abigail had recklessly lied to him about her age, adding an additional two years to her seventeen. They'd fallen in love, and she'd loved him with a love beyond her years. She'd grown up instantly, as women sometimes do when they fall desperately in love. Their love had known no bounds, and she'd unwisely surrendered herself completely to him, believing that he would inevitably marry her. All through the summer she put off telling him her age; she stalled him when he demanded that they drive into Pittsburgh and talk to her parents. She knew they would object strongly, and she was too afraid to lose him. Finally their love had led to the most wonderful of nights, when he'd made her his own.

Abigail's smile was a tight, painful line as she continued to reflect.

She saw Grant and herself walking hand in hand in the woods. Her golden hair flowed over her shoulders to her waist. She'd twined wild flowers in its thickness, and their scent was sweetly enveloping. Grant stopped suddenly and took her in his arms. He looked down at her, his black eyes shining tenderly. In the darkness his thick hair seemed almost black, his skin as swarthy as the light brown earth. She thought him the most handsome man in the world. He took one of her hands in his. His voice—never in the eight years that had passed had Abigail forgotten the deep, rich, musical sound of it—caressed her as he reverently vowed he would belong to her forever.

"I love you, Abigail. You're the only woman I'll ever love."

And eagerly she vowed the same, with only the vast outdoors and creatures of the woods as witnesses. It had been the most beautiful of moments. Then on the exact spot where they had promised themselves to each other, they consummated their love. Grant drew her down onto a bed of soft grasses and made her his with passionate completeness.

She could still remember the molten glory of their bodies touching that first time, the thrill and delight of the newness of him, the wondrous, building excitement, and finally the dazzling eruption of every sense in her being.

"Abigail, you didn't hear a word I was saying," Rosalind interrupted impatiently. "What were you thinking of?"

"Grant…and…the last time I saw him."

"Him!" Rosalind hissed in utter disgust. "I haven't forgotten him either! I can't believe you'd think of him when you have a man like Harold."

"I don't know why I did…really."

"I'll never forgive myself for what happened," Rosalind said. "What could have possessed me to send you up to my sister's that summer?"

"In another age I would have been a ruined woman—and at seventeen!" Abigail mused, realizing that was scarcely the proper thing to say.

"Nonsense! In another age I would have made him marry you!"

"And he would have!" Abigail's voice softened unaccountably at the thought.

"He wanted to sleep with you, and he wanted your money. I told you that he took money when I offered it to him to leave you alone."

"I didn't leave him! You took me away!"

"For your own good! And it was a little late in the day. You were already pregnant."

"How could he have found me anyway? You sent me to Texas to have the baby."

Abigail would never forget those long months of agony before her baby's future had been settled. She'd wanted to keep her child, and her mother had wanted to put the baby out for adoption with strangers. Finally, when Michael was born, Lisa, Abigail's older sister, and her husband had pleaded that they wanted to adopt him. It had been a compromise, but only that. Abigail had missed him terribly the moment she'd handed him into her sister's arms, but she couldn't keep him if she couldn't offer him his father's name.

Two years ago Lisa and Ed had been killed in a car wreck on a European vacation. Rosalind had been named in their will as Michael's temporary guardian until Abigail married. Only when Abigail married was she to become Michael's guardian. Only then would her son be her own.

Abigail remembered the terrible boarding schools that had followed her pregnancy.

"That was such an unhappy time," Abigail murmured.

"It wasn't easy for any of us, let me assure you, darling."

"Those schools were so strict I never saw a male younger than feeble old Uncle Ned, and he was eighty and in a nursing home."

"You're exaggerating!"

"Not much." Abigail sighed, remembering those

awful years. She'd lived like a prisoner shut away from the world.

"I knew Peggy was eccentric, but it just never occurred to me that she wouldn't look after you properly that summer. Why, you were half-wild when I got you back, and crazy about that... that...child molester."

"He thought I was nineteen!"

"I've never believed that! You hardly look nineteen now, even though you're twenty-five! And to think my own sister...I couldn't believe Peggy took that monster's side completely."

"That...monster...was the gentlest—" Abigail broke off, startled that she was actually defending Grant. "Mother, I...I know what I did was wrong, but in all these years there's never been another man that..." She couldn't quite come out and admit that she was frigid. Talking to Rosalind on so intimate a topic was not easy. "...that made me feel like he did. Not even Harold. Sometimes I wonder if I can make Harold happy...as a woman."

"You were seventeen, darling. That was your first experience. You're grown-up now. You can't expect to feel like you did when you were a child. You and Harold will grow to love each other in a more mature way. You shouldn't compare Harold or yourself to a...a memory. Oh, I'll never forgive myself for that dreadful summer. You wouldn't be having these doubts now. You'd know how lucky were you to catch a fine, upright young man like him. You wouldn't have to feel guilty that you aren't a virgin.''

"Oh, I certainly don't feel guilty about that!''

Rosalind's stiff, condescending gaze swept her daughter. That was the very kind of statement she found most alarming. Just when she thought she had Abigail well in hand, Abigail always burst out with the wrong thing. Thankfully, she was so beautiful, Harold hadn't noticed this lamentable failing. "Darling, just thinking about all this makes me glad that Peggy isn't coming to the wedding. She might do— or say—something that wouldn't be at all suitable.''

"Aunt Peggy isn't coming?''

"She called this morning to say—'' Suddenly Rosalind's voice was slightly agitated. "Well, never mind what she said.''

"What exactly did she say, Mother?'' Abigail's gaze was firm.

"Well, you know how she thinks all weddings are dreadful bores, and she doesn't approve of Harold, so you can't take a thing she says on the subject seriously.''

"What did she say?''

"That she didn't want to be present when I auctioned you off to the highest bidder. That you'd never be happy a day in your life if you married into that pompous, cold family. Can you imagine saying that about the Harrisons?'' Rosalind's tone was one of horror, as though she considered what her sister had said sacrilegious.

"Don't worry, Mother. I don't think Aunt Peggy is very reverent, even when it comes to much more established institutions than the Harrisons,'' Abigail retorted dryly, determined to call her aunt as soon as she returned to her studio apartment on the other side of town and could be assured of privacy. Her mother seemed very nervous suddenly, and Abigail had the strangest feeling that Rosalind was not telling her everything.

A feeble ray of gray sunlight sifted through the skylight of Abigail's studio apartment. Holding the receiver of her cordless telephone tightly against her ear, Abigail moved purposefully toward the full-length mirror that hung on one wall. The telephone had been a gift from the very efficient Rosalind, who'd long ago decided that Abigail wasted far too much time on the phone. Since she couldn't nag her daughter into changing her habit, Rosalind had instructed Abigail at least to do her housework or paint while she talked.

She let the phone ring for at least five minutes. That didn't necessarily mean Peggy wasn't home. Joslynn, her aunt's estate, was enormous, and her

Aunt Peggy could simply be too far from the phone to hear it. Besides, Aunt Peggy had the most maddening habit of letting the phone ring when she wasn't in the mood to answer it. But the longer it rang, the better the chance that her curiosity would get the better of her and she would answer it.

Abigail began to scrub furiously at a blob of paint on the mirror's surface. Possessing an artist's mania for light, she'd hung mirrors all over the tiny apartment the day after she'd moved in two years ago.

There! The blob was gone! Now to attack the clutter littering her home—the stacked canvases, the tangle of clothes she had to step over, and the unwashed dishes spilling over the sink onto the countertop. The place was a wreck! Normally she was a fair housekeeper; things had only gotten this bad because her every waking moment had been spent on preparations for her wedding.

She surveyed the disaster, sorry in spite of the mess, that she would be moving out. She felt free here. She would have to see if Harold relented and at least allowed her to keep her studio here. He was determined that she have a studio in a more fashionable part of town, and she was sure he would be equally determined that she keep it in perfect order. Harold despised irregularities.

She pushed Harold and his fussy orderliness from her mind, picked up a large paint-spattered canvas and headed toward the enormous cabinet that she'd had built especially to store her canvases. The telephone was still pressed to her ear.

"Hello!" barked a crisp, out-of-breath voice in a tone so startling that Abigail nearly dropped the receiver.

"Aunt Peggy! I thought you weren't going to answer. This is—"

"I know. I know. I was outside when the phone started ringing, and when I opened the door, Roar got out along with Benji and Fuzzy. It's been chaos, dear, keeping the others inside while I corralled those three rascals."

Aunt Peggy loved animals and had so many pets that no one but she could keep track of them. Abigail knew Roar was a German shepherd and Fuzzy a great indignant white Persian, but she couldn't remember Benji.

"If I called at a bad time…"

"No, dear, I wanted to talk to you, and I've been trying to get you for days."

"Mother's been keeping me very busy."

"I thought as much. Finally, in desperation I even called her and asked her to have you call me."

Abigail remembered her mother's strange nervousness. "She didn't mention you called to talk to me."

"She's never trusted me since… Well, you know.

Anyway, I imagine she wants you safely married to that…that Haroldson.''

"Harold Harrison."

"Whoever. Anyway since she knows I detest the idea of your marrying into a family like that, she doesn't want to risk our having anything to do with one another until after the wedding.''

"But what could you possibly do or say that would frighten Mother?''

This question was followed by a pregnant silence. When Aunt Peggy spoke again, her voice sounded strange.

"I'm afraid I have the most frightful news, dear. I've struggled with my conscience for days, but no matter how angry I make Rosalind, I can't play God—even for her sake.''

"Aunt Peggy, what is it?''

"Grant has come back. He's bought the house he stayed in all those years ago, and he wants to see you again. He's so changed, dear. I think you'd better come up here immediately, before he does something rash.''

"Rash?''

"He's determined to see you—one way or the other. I can't answer for what he'll do, if you don't.''

Two

Abigail held the buzzing receiver in her hand. She felt curiously dazed. After eight years, Grant had come back, and he was demanding to see her again. What could it mean? From what Aunt Peggy had said, he didn't sound like the gentle lover she'd known, but a harsh and arrogant stranger.

Still, she'd known from the first moment her aunt had told her that he was back that she would go to Joslynn to see him. She had to, not only because he demanded it, but because there was no telling what he might do. In the first place, he didn't know about Michael. When Rosalind had told him about the expected baby eight years ago, he hadn't wanted any part of his child. Rosalind had subsequently decided it wisest to tell him that Abigail had miscarried. Besides the danger of him discovering he had a son, there was the worry that he might say something to Harold.

Abigail thought uneasily of her mother and how terribly upset Rosalind would be if she knew Abigail was planning to see Grant again. Rosalind thought that she had everything under control. With her usual scrupulous attention to detail, Rosalind had planned practically every minute of her daughter's life for the coming fourteen days. There was a shower tonight and a party at the country club tomorrow. Abigail knew her calendar was covered with appointments and engagements. Rosalind, who was benign and even affectionate when she had her way, would be livid if Abigail evaded even one of these commitments. Abigail knew her mother would have preferred to handle this threat herself, just as she'd handled Grant long ago when Abigail had been too upset to do so. Rosalind wasn't going to understand why Abigail now felt she had to do this herself.

But nothing, not even Rosalind's displeasure, mattered when Abigail thought of seeing Grant again. It was something she had to do herself.

Hastily, Abigail scribbled a note that really didn't explain anything to her mother. She deliberately omitted the most pertinent details: her real destination as well as her reason for leaving. She knew Rosalind would follow her if she told her where she was going. So Abigail wrote only that something of importance had come up and that she had to go away for a few days to take care of it.

She wrote in a wildly rambling fashion across the front of a sheet of drawing paper, then squeezed her signature into one corner and placed the note in the center of her kitchen table, propped between a jar of peanut butter and a can of peaches. In afterthought, Abigail asked her mother to call Harold and explain.

Rosalind would be in a rage by the time she finished reading the note, and Abigail felt sorry about that. But she couldn't think what to write to spare her mother anxiety.

Quickly she threw some clothes and a few toilet articles into a suitcase. Then she locked the door and hurried down to the garage and climbed into her Volkswagen.

Abigail drove through winding golden hills, noting nothing about her beautiful hometown except the traffic signs and signals to which she mechanically responded. A tourist traveling the same roads might have reflected that this magnificent city of three mighty rivers, where the flowing waters of the Allegheny and the Monongahela met to form the Ohio

River, this city known by many names—the Steel City, the City of Bridges, the Gateway to the West— was a city of immense raw power.

Steel mills stretched for miles along the river banks. Behind the sparkling rivers and the graceful lawns of Point State Park and the jet streams of the Point Fountain, modern buildings jutted against the bleak sky. The world headquarters of such giants as Gulf Oil, U.S. Steel, Alcoa, PPG and Westinghouse were housed in these downtown glass skyscrapers. Every day, Abigail's own father participated in corporate intrigue in these ''Fortune 500'' boardrooms.

Abigail's mind was focused on Grant and not on her executive father or Pittsburgh, this city of sharp contrasts, of great wealth as well of abject poverty. Famed for such industrial magnates as Andrew Carnegie, Henry Clay Frick, Henry C. Phipps, George Westinghouse and Thomas Mellon, Pittsburgh was proud of her successful sons, and they returned her love with generous philanthropic gifts. Like most other Pittsburgh natives, Abigail had always taken these museums, numerous endowments, libraries, art galleries and parks for granted.

Not all of Pittsburgh's sons were rich. On the south side of the city, far from the lush parks and glamorous display of wealth, the steel mills were a gigantic, teeming sprawl. Generations of steelworkers lived there in squalor, in frame houses perched haphazardly on the hillsides—"clingers" in local parlance.

A product of her hometown, Abigail was the pampered daughter of a mighty industrialist who had made a brilliant marriage to Rosalind Blake; whose family had amassed a fortune in the Pennsylvania oil boom several decades earlier. Grant Nichols, too, was a child of Pittsburgh, but not a rich one. He was the son of a poor Irish family, second generation steelworkers who scarcely managed to eke out a living in the belching furnaces that flourished upstream.

Rain was beginning to fall lightly. Abigail switched on the windshield wipers, which slashed jerkily across the glass, smearing several drops of rain. As she drove she was oblivious to the familiar surroundings—to the gold dome of a Greek Orthodox church peeping from behind a cluster of scarlet trees, to the sandstone cliffs topped with quaint and charming turn-of-the-century houses with steep pitched roofs and broad porches. Nor did she see the gorgeous fall colors that flamed like a brilliant collage of red, gold and brown against the hills. Instead, she drove with determination, speeding onto the freeway and joining the thread of cars heading east. Great orange earth movers and other heavy equipment blocked off one lane of the highway, and Abigail sighed with frustration as the traffic slowed.

Thirty miles later she turned off the freeway onto a narrow macadam road that twisted beneath golden trees through low wooded hills. Orchards fringed the roadside. In the spring, this stretch of road was dazzling with beautifully fragrant, lacy apple blossoms, the trees astir with hummingbirds and bees, soft flower petals fluttering in the slightest breeze. In late summer and fall the same trees were festooned with tangy, crimson apples.

The road was rain-slicked and badly in need of repairs. The Volkswagen bumped along, but Abigail scarcely noticed the jolting. She was in a daze of worry, wondering what Grant intended to do.

Twilight gave way to darkness, and Abigail drove on in the thick rain toward Aunt Peggy's. The hours dragged wearily by.

By midnight Abigail had been on the narrow, twisting road for nearly four hours. It was a black, moonless night. The rain was falling in sheets. Visibility was so poor that she hunched over the steering wheel like an awkward crane to peer into the darkness. Her neck was cramped from the strain of this posture, and her eyes burned.

Abigail's stomach rumbled. She had skipped lunch, and for supper she'd eaten only a small sack of peanuts and drunk a Coke when she'd stopped for gas. At the time she hadn't been hungry.

She cracked her window an inch, and cold drops

of rain gusted inside. She smelled the damp woodsy odor she associated with Aunt Peggy's. If she hadn't been so tired and hungry, it would have been heavenly.

Oh, when was she going to be at Aunt Peggy's? It couldn't be too much farther. She'd just gone through the last village seven miles ago.

Abigail scanned the darkness for Joslynn's gilded gates. Aunt Peggy would be expecting her and would have a warm cup of tea and a blazing fire. Abigail looked forward to her aunt's soothing, if zany company.

As she sped past an opening in the trees, she slowed the car. In the beam of the headlights she saw the familiar sign sagging on its listing post. She wondered if it now read Nichols.

Grant's cottage was down that dirt road, which was scarcely more than a path now. A tiny light flickered at the end of the unpaved road. Something in the pit of her stomach rolled uneasily, and she was aware of a faint tense feeling.

Years ago the sight of a light burning in his cottage would have afforded her intense excitement. She would have been thrilled at the thought of him at home. The years had slipped away, and now her heart beat strangely fast. But she forced herself to drive on, knowing that in less than a quarter of a mile she would reach the familiar gates to her aunt's estate.

Soon the massive gates came into view. Braking the car again, she opened the car door. A blast of rain sprayed water over her like a cold shower. She had to get out to call her aunt on the intercom to open the gates. With no raincoat to shield herself, she plunged out into the chill, wet fury. Her fine leather shoes crunched into mud and gravel and ruin. In seconds her faded jeans and long-sleeved T-shirt were soaked through.

Crouching over the little box and pressing the button, she screamed into the microphone again and again with no result. Was it broken? Or was her aunt merely in some remote part of the vast house? The wind shivered through the trees, and Abigail began to shake with cold. She couldn't stand out here all night. She would have to think of some other way to contact her aunt.

Abigail sank back in the driver's seat and slammed the door. Cold water trickled in icy rivulets along her scalp and down her neck. Her soaked clothes clung in sopping layers to her body. She was dripping all over the upholstery and carpet, but she was too miserable to care.

She felt tired as well. The rounds of parties, the emotional strain of it all, the long drive…and now this. Her teeth began to chatter, and she laid her head wearily against the cold plastic steering wheel.

She shuddered as a series of tremors shook her. Frozen solid—that's how she felt! She couldn't stay in this car a minute longer. It was too late to drive back to the village. When she'd driven through half an hour earlier, the town had been dark save for a single street-light that emitted only the feeblest ray in the swirling rain. There was nothing for it but to go back to Grant's house and hope he was there and she could call her aunt.

At the thought of going to Grant's house, her heart began to pound with startling ferocity. This wasn't exactly the way she'd pictured their first meeting. She didn't want to see him, not when she was so exhausted and he was not expecting her. Despite her misgivings, she turned the key, and the car engine roared into life.

Deliberately, she pushed Grant from her mind. She was glad suddenly of small comforts—of the heater blasting her with its warmth, of the dryness of the enclosed car. Rain continued to fall in a freezing downpour.

She turned onto the bumpy unpaved road that wound to the cottage. Abigail was oblivious to the gothic overtones—the violent storm, the dark forest, a young woman in trouble alone. She was too physically uncomfortable to be afraid that anyone sinister lurked in the forest or in the cottage at the end of the road. Besides, even a ghoulish hunchback would be a welcome sight if his mood were hospitable and he had a dry house and offered her a hot cup of tea.

The house came into view. The windows were brilliant squares of light. Through the rain she made out the blurry outlines of the house itself, and it was just as she remembered—a tiny, cozy sandstone cottage with a steep timbered roof.

For a long time she sat in her car, dreading to get out and knock on the door. What would he do? What would he say? What could she possibly say to him? She began to tremble from the cold again.

The bright little square lights beckoned her. Finally she summoned her courage and heaved herself out into the rain and ran toward the protection of the dark porch. She knocked timidly on the door. Her knock was too feeble to be heard above the rushing waterfall that poured from the gutter. When no one answered, she pounded against the storm door more loudly.

"Don't break the glass, love," a man's voice called out.

Abigail heard the heavy tread of a man's boots resounding on stone floors. The door was thrust open. The musical male voice that she remembered so well wrapped her with the velvet softness of passionate welcome. "Sweetheart, I didn't really expect you tonight…what with this storm and all. But there's no need to break the door down. Don't waste your energy when we've got the whole night…''

The whispery male voice stirred disturbing memories of his virility. She gasped, not knowing what to do. It was too late to escape, but she felt so uncertain. She wasn't sure she could face him.

It was the sexual innuendo in his husky voice that alarmed her. An onslaught of nerves made Abigail shiver even more violently.

Grant switched the porch light on, and she was momentarily blinded by the unexpected brilliance.

''You're not—'' His tone had changed, and she realized he had been expecting someone else. The welcome in his voice was gone. In its place was surprise and a new hardness. ''Abbie! Is that…? You are Abigail Bainbridge?''

Even as she registered the shock in his deep cold tone, she nodded.

''What are you doing here?'' Black, smoldering eyes ran over her.

Her damp blouse was like transparent gauze plastered to the seductive curve of her ripe, voluptuous breasts.

''You said you wanted to see me, Grant,'' she said weakly, aware of his gaze traveling downward from her breasts to her thighs and shapely legs that were clearly revealed by her clinging jeans. If only he wouldn't look at her like that! She felt strangely hot even as she shivered.

She wished that for just this once she'd put on something more suitable.

Slowly and with deliberate insolence he ran his gaze upward, assessing every female curve with such shattering avidity it was all she could do not to slap him. At last his hot black eyes met her furious blue ones.

"I damn sure didn't expect you on my doorstep tonight," he said, sucking in a deep, hard breath just as she did the same.

"Obviously. And I didn't think I'd wind up here tonight myself." Her voice trembled with rage. "I didn't want to see you! You're the last person... But I had no choice. You see—"

He cut her off. "Save your insults! What about Mama and that millionaire fiancé of yours? Do they know where you are?"

"No. I didn't tell anyone I was coming here."

"So, you've come alone without telling anybody, not even Mama. I wonder why."

"You can quit wondering!" she sputtered, realizing her mistake instantly to have admitted no one knew where she was.

She felt desperate. She searched his eyes for a shred of sympathy, but she found no mercy. Instead he threw back his dark head and laughed, but it was not the warm sound she remembered loving. It was harsh, and it grated on her nerves. A chill tingled unpleasantly down her spine.

"You're still the same coward you were eight years ago, Abbie," he began. "Afraid of honesty and real emotions and real people, tied to all the warped values of your class."

"My class! You say that as if I'm not a human being but some sort of robot!"

"That's exactly what you are."

Her fury blazed as hotly as his. "Damn you! Who are you to judge me? You don't even know me! You never did!" She stopped herself before she gave into her own bitterness.

"Oh, that's where you're wrong." A cruel, suggestive element had crept into his deep voice. "I was the first to know you, remember?"

For an instant the poignant memory of their one night of uninhibited lovemaking was too vividly clear. "I've tried very very hard to forget," she sputtered, feeling a terrible pain at his gibe.

"That figures. You couldn't face the honesty of that night, could you, Abbie? You're like a beautiful wooden doll—lovely to look at but hollow inside."

Hollow—if only she'd been that, perhaps he couldn't have hurt her so deeply.

He was staring at her hard as though he were

really seeing her for the first time tonight. "Beautiful?" He muttered the word questioningly.

The mockery in his last word made her acutely aware of her appearance, and she turned as furiously purple as a plum. The poised Abigail Bainbridge shouldn't run around in the middle of the night garbed in a see-through filmy T-shirt that shamelessly revealed her body. His words about her polished, doll-like beauty were ironic, but no more so than her presence on his doorstep.

He lifted his gaze from the angry rise and fall of her breasts, and his knowing eyes met hers.

"Don't say anything!" she said. "I know I don't look too great right now."

His hostile manner eased, and his eyes lit with the faintest hint of the devilish glint she remembered so well as his sense of humor prevailed over his other darker emotions. "That's an understatement, if there ever was one. The fact is you look more like a soggy raccoon than a beautiful doll."

"I feel like one, too," she said lamely. "I didn't expect you to welcome me with open arms. But I feel awful, and it doesn't help—your slinging insults, calling me names and making fun of me."

"I was blasting away at you with both guns, wasn't I?" he asked.

She felt an odd disappointment that Grant should see her so bedraggled. Though she took a certain

pride in her appearance, normally she wasn't vain.
But in that moment she was acutely so.

The wind and the rain had demolished her hair,
matting it into clumps that fell over her brows, one
lump dangling over her right ear like a sodden tail.
Her clothes clung like soaked rags to her figure, revealing every detail of her feminine shape. His gaze
lingered on her full rounded breasts at the exact spot
where the tips of her nipples pushed against the thin
damp material of her shirt, and she wished fervently
that she'd worn a bra. He must think her a dishev-
eled wreck. While he…

He looked magnificent, if one went for tall, darkly
handsome males who were so virile that they made
one's toes curl and sent delicious tingles shivering
down one's spine. Unfortunately, that seemed to be
exactly what she went for. Suddenly she was shivering again and more fiercely than ever, but that was
only because it was practically freezing, she told
herself furiously. And he smelled good, too. She
caught his fresh masculine scent mingling with his
tangy after-shave. Her eyes slowly traveled up his
body, from his narrow hips over his flat stomach to
his lean muscular torso. He hadn't put on a single
pound. She hated the curious breathlessness that
swept her, but she told herself it was only the damp
and cold that made her feel so strange, not the sheer
perfection of his male body.

His hair, dark auburn and rumpled, fell untidily across his brow, giving him a rakish air. He was unchanged except for the grooves beside his sensual mouth and the tiny lines beneath his eyes. There was a new cynicism in his expression that hadn't been there before. He was deeply tanned. She wondered idly where one acquired a tan in October. Nevertheless, he was devastatingly handsome.

A faded blue cotton work shirt spanned the massive breadth of his shoulders. The collar was frayed at the edges, and she was reminded that he'd always preferred old clothes. Several buttons had been left unbuttoned, revealing a disturbing strip of dark flesh covered with black hair. He wore blue jeans that molded his muscular thighs.

"I always thought stripping gazes were a man's prerogative," his deep voice mocked, and she flushed bright red. "Here, let me show you how it's done." His flashing black eyes swept over her with a bold intimacy that made her go hot all over in spite of the fact she was chilled to the bone. Again his black gaze paused where her thrusting breasts made her thin shirt rise and fall.

A hot current flowed through her. She was momentarily mesmerized.

He smiled boldly down at her. She noted that his teeth were straight and white against his dark skin. He was as handsome as ever, and he knew it.

"Don't look at me like that!" she cried at last, recovering herself, remembering that these were the treacherous feelings that once had led to the destruction of her life.

"Why not? You were devouring me with your eyes! And if I don't mind, why should you?"

"I wasn't doing it...like you were."

"But that was only because you lack the proper experience." He shot her an amused grin. "In a few more lessons you'll be the expert I am."

"You look...you are...ridiculously conceited," she managed, wanting to wipe the confident look from his swarthy features.

The baldly confident look was as impudent as the rest of him, and it refused to be erased.

"You know, Abigail," he said easily, "I think I like the way you look tonight, without your polish and paint and society outfits. At least you look very real."

"Do you think I care what you think?"

They stared at one another for a long, silent moment.

"So what brings you here tonight, princess?" he asked, his voice hardening.

A chill swept her, and she began to shake. "As if you didn't know! It's your fault I'm here. Aunt Peggy called and said you were making threats. I certainly didn't come to see you because I wanted to! Right now I need to use your phone to call Aunt Peggy.'' A new rush of anger swept through her at what she considered his arrogance and rudeness, and she failed to note the quick look of pain he suppressed. "I'm freezing!" she stated furiously. "Are you going to make me stand out here all night?"

"The thought occurred to me that it's exactly what you deserve."

Not a shred of her cool, careful Bainbridge reserve remained. She wanted to kick him in the shin. Just when her patience was about to snap, he relented.

"Won't you come in?" he offered with mock gallantry, bowing gracefully toward her as though she were indeed a princess.

Summoning the last vestige of her pride, she stepped inside. Not daring to glance at him, she drew a shaky hand through her hair, brushing back the tumbling masses of damp gold. He watched this alluring, feminine gesture. She could feel the hot intensity of his gaze, and it made her uncomfortable.

He would think it odd if she couldn't look at him. Feeling embarrassed, she glared up at him from a safe distance, masking her tumultuous feelings with anger.

"I might have drowned out there waiting for you to invite me inside," she snapped.

He smiled lazily. "No chance of that. I was more

than willing to perform mouth to mouth resuscitation.''

Her gaze flitted to his full sensual mouth, curving slightly with ill-repressed amusement. Then she looked quickly away, annoyed at herself, but not before she was again aware of her own treacherous response to him as a man. ''I think I'd almost prefer to drown,'' she muttered, believing that fate less dangerous.

''I doubt it,'' was all he said, but his smile and the bold knowledge in his expression said much more.

She ignored the insolent gleam in his black eyes. Her anger drained away. She was much too tired for intense emotion. She moved farther into the room toward the orange glow that leapt in the grate, radiating the most delicious warmth she'd ever felt.

He observed her, acutely conscious of the exquisite feminine grace in her every movement, in the gently swaying motion of her hips, in the light quickness of her steps.

When she reached the fire she hunkered down in front of it and continued to shiver. Water pooled on the warm stone floor beneath her. Her pale skin glowed golden in the firelight, her blue eyes were luminous.

Grant stood watching her for a long moment, stunned by the mixture of emotions he was feeling.

She appeared so tiny and helpless, so young and vulnerable, and she hadn't lost that funny little lost look he'd adored. She was as hauntingly lovely as he remembered, as vibrantly passionate as the first night she'd surrendered to his love.

He'd thought he'd feel his old fierce anger when he saw her again, but instead he felt something entirely different. The past and all its pain was there between them, and yet...

She turned toward him before he had time to fully analyze his strange emotion.

"Well, are you just going to stand there gawking at me like that for the rest of the night?" Blue eyes sparked indignantly. Her expression was pert. The warmth of the fire was obviously restoring her energy and her zest. Some of the color had come back into her cheeks.

A smile tugged at the corner of his lips as he regarded her. "Sorry. You take some getting used to, you know," he said dryly. "What do you say we call a truce?"

"I say that's a capital idea, if you'll stick to it," she agreed with a faint, taunting smile.

"I'll go to the bathroom and get some towels."

After eight years she was back in his life as if she'd never left it, and somehow, though he knew it was all wrong, it felt very right. When he returned, he handed her a fluffy stack of freshly laundered towels. He knelt and spread two thick blankets before the fire.

"Thanks."

"You're welcome."

Sinking down onto the blankets, she began vigorously toweling her hair. But all of her attention was focused on his lean handsomeness as he bent over and tossed another log on the fire. She watched the material of his blue shirt ripple across his muscular back.

"Anything else I can do for you, princess?" he offered as he closed the black screen of the fireplace.

"You can stop calling me princess! And I would simply love a cup of hot tea."

When his eyes met hers, they were so black and intense that she felt warm and shivery all in the same moment. But when he spoke, his tone was mild. "Okay."

He left, and she continued to dry her hair, all the while very aware of the sounds coming from the kitchen. He was certainly going to a lot of trouble to make a single cup of tea. Men could be so helpless in the kitchen, she decided with feminine conceit, though Grant hardly looked the helpless type anywhere else.

When she heard cabinet doors being opened and slammed, the refrigerator door opening and closing, and china clattering, a tiny smile of amusement curved her lips as she imagined his frustration. But she resisted the impulse to help him. Only when the tea kettle whistled, did she rise and amble into the kitchen to see how he'd managed.

"What are you doing?" she asked, instantly realizing he was certainly not helpless in the kitchen. He'd done far more than prepare a simple cup of tea. In a glance she saw the kitchen table was neatly set for one, and that he was removing a plate of steaming pot roast and vegetables from the microwave. She hadn't cooked a meal like that—ever!

The kitchen was freshly painted a bright white and so immaculately kept that she flinched with shame at the thought of the shambles of her own apartment. Starched blue and white gingham curtains decorated the back wall of windows. Formica surfaces gleamed, and guiltily she remembered her own sticky countertops. She admired his obvious housekeeping talent so immensely that, had he been a woman, she could easily have detested him for making her so acutely aware of her own deficiencies in that department.

"I thought you might be hungry," he returned pleasantly. "It's a long drive from Pittsburgh in this kind of weather."

"I didn't want to put you to all this trouble," she mumbled, reaching for the cup of tea and feeling suddenly embarrassed. "I don't usually barge in on people in the middle of the night expecting to be fed.''

"I know you don't," he said softly. There was a new element in his deep voice, and again just the way he looked at her caused every nerve in her body to tingle.

"I only wanted to use your phone."

"That can wait 'til after you've eaten."

"I couldn't reach Aunt Peggy on the intercom," she started to explain.

"Eat," he commanded, watching her intently.

Sinking into the kitchen chair in front of the plate of food, she picked up the slice of lemon in her saucer and squeezed it. "This really is nice of you," she said, feeling awkward and nervous.

"There's nothing I like better than being nice," he mocked silkily.

There was something cozily intimate about sharing a kitchen with a man, and she was reminded of other intimacies they had shared. A strange aura of danger pervaded the room.

"It's just leftovers from supper," he said casually.

The aroma from the thick juicy roast wafted in the air, and her stomach growled with enthusiasm. "It smells delicious, and I…I'm not just hungry, I'm starved."

He leaned back against the stove and smiled down

at her as she carved a piece of roast beef. "I seem to remember eating was always something you put off until you were famished."

"I didn't stop on the road for dinner because I didn't want to take the time. I was in such a hurry."

"You haven't changed," he said quietly.

She lifted her gaze to his darkly handsome features, and for an instant her breath caught in her throat.

"Neither have you."

The words were out of her mouth even before she realized she'd spoken. She glanced up. Her eyes met his, and even though she wanted to look away, she couldn't. His awesome virility was compelling. She devoured him visually as though she'd been starved for the sight of him. Time seemed to slide backward, and all the old powerful feelings swirled around her. She felt hot and cold, aflame with strange erotic sensations.

The answering blaze of passion she saw in his black eyes jolted her, and she was trembling. He was so tall, so vitally masculine. He towered over her, filling the kitchen with his male presence. His dark intense gaze never left her face, and she felt as she'd felt all those years ago—completely his, spiritually as well as physically. Her pulse pounded crazily, and in spite of her damp clothes, she was on fire with a strange heat that radiated from within. He made no move toward her, no attempt to touch her, and yet with his eyes he touched every intimate place of her body, touching even her heart and soul.

"No," she cried softly, wanting to deny the intense feelings he could so effortlessly evoke.

She felt dizzy, as though she might faint—she who had never fainted in all of her life! Her fingers gripped the edge of the table. She was aware of how powerfully attracted she felt to him, and she knew too well the danger of those feelings.

"Grant…I…I…" Her words broke the strange spell that bound them together. "This is just a crazy mistake."

"Is it?" he asked huskily.

"We mustn't."

"Oh, but you're so wrong."

In the grip of an odd panic, she pushed herself from the table. "It's late, and I really don't think I should be here."

She heard his low chuckle. "Probably not, but since you are…"

He spanned the short distance that separated them, and suddenly she was in his arms. Strong hands gripped her, and when she offered no resistance, they slid down her back, shaping her feminine curves to his own aroused body. She tried to wedge her hands between his shoulders and her own body, but his chest was like a solid, immovable rock.

"Don't!" She struggled in earnest.

His rough cheek grazed her temple, and she caught the spicy scent of his after-shave and the familiar scent that was distinctly his. His fingers moved beneath her damp shirt, spreading across the bare flesh of her back, pressing her body even more closely to his. She felt the incredible heat of him enveloping her, and old erotic memories stirred.

"You feel so good," he murmured hoarsely, his breath tickling as he brushed the sensitive flesh beside her ear with his warm lips. "And you still taste as delicious as ever," his low voice teased.

She twisted her head frantically to evade his exploring mouth. He only laughed softly at her futile attempts to avoid his kisses. He was a man who'd grown up with women, a man who knew all their weaknesses, especially hers. He was a man who'd grown up on the wrong side of the tracks, a man who'd learned early he had to fight for what he wanted.

"Grant, don't. Please. You mustn't."

"You never used to say no, Abbie. What are you so afraid of all of a sudden?" His weight was pressing her backward against the wall. Solid male flesh imprisoned her.

"I..." She couldn't speak. Strange, confused feelings bombarded every sense in her being. His nearness and his caresses were an emotional assault she didn't know how to combat. Tempestuous excitement and desire laced with a vague sensation of danger coursed through her. Her fragile strength was nothing compared to his.

She knew that things were happening too fast, that she was getting in too deep too quickly with the one man of all men she shouldn't trust. But he made her feel so divinely sensual, so completely female that it was difficult to think at all. Her fingers curled against his tough, hard muscle. She could only gaze breathlessly up into his dark fathomless eyes.

He had asked her what she was afraid of.

"This?" His male voice seemed to wrap around her, the one word low and seductive.

His hand curved along her slender throat, gently tilting her exquisite face toward his. For an instant she stopped breathing, and then she closed her eyes as his mouth deliberately descended to possess hers.

Three

"**W**ill you let me go?" Abigail blazed, her voice strangely tight and breathless. She pushed against Grant's shoulders with her hands, straining with all her might to free herself from his iron grip. He caught her to him, arching the lower part of her body against his, so that she was imprisoned even more intimately than before.

"What did you come in here for," Grant demanded roughly, "if you didn't want this? It's after midnight. You're braless in a see-through shirt that reveals more than it conceals."

"It's wet," Abigail hissed. "And it got that way accidentally."

"All I know is how damned sexy you look in it," he growled huskily. "I'm a man, not a statue made of stone."

She was all too aware of the truth of that statement as he crushed her against the vibrant warmth of his vital male body. He cupped her chin with his hand, and then his mouth closed over her parted lips in a long, drugging kiss. She was aware of his hands roaming over her body, of buttons being loosened—whether they were hers or his she didn't know—of damp fabric sliding away so that warm flesh fitted against warm flesh.

Through the wetness of her T-shirt she could feel the thudding beat of his heart. Her breasts were flattened against the hard warmth of his chest. She strained against him, but he used her every movement to mold her body more closely to his. Slowly her fear subsided, and in its place a glowing heat spread.

She opened her mouth, and his tongue thrust inside to taste the velvet sweetness of her mouth. She was like a rare wine, moist and delicious and heady. He drank deeply, as though he'd thirsted for her for eight years. And like a man who'd been too long without a drink, the first taste went to his head. After that first sip, he was beyond stopping himself.

His kisses were long and sensual. Molten fire raced through her veins, and her bones seemed to melt with the heat of her complete arousal. She was limp and unresisting when he lifted her into his arms and carried her into the living room. Gently he placed her body on the blankets spread before the roaring fire.

The weight of his body pressed her down to the floor. Vaguely she was aware of him removing her jeans. The heat of his embrace made her feel strangely languorous. She knew she should resist, but her will to do so had drained away. Every sense in her body was aflame with desire. He was temptation, and like Eve in the garden of Eden, she was fatally attracted.

He ripped off his shirt, and her hands ran over his rippling, hard, brown muscles. It had been so long. She exulted in the tense warmth of his flesh, in his closeness. She wanted to touch every inch of him, to give him the same pleasure with her light caresses that he was giving her.

She trembled violently as he pushed her shirt over her head, as his hands glided over the curve of her breasts. Her nipples grew erect and taut, and gently he lowered his head to fondle them with his lips. She was fleetingly aware of danger at the boldness of his new intimacy, but as a thousand delicious sensations shivered through her, her anxieties were pushed to the back of her mind. She was aware only of how wildly wanton, how totally alive and feminine his mere touch could make her feel.

His hot mouth moved across her lush soft breasts to nuzzle the warm hollow between them. Pagan needs exploded within her, and she clasped her hands around his neck, pressing him even more closely against herself. The violence of her emotion was overwhelming, and she felt herself drowning in wave after wave of ever stronger sensations. She was his—only his. It had always been so since that first moment when she'd met him. He had only to look at her, to touch her, and she was his to possess.

She moaned, straining toward him, her own aching need so intense that she felt she would die from exquisite torture if he didn't make her his completely.

"Oh, Grant, I want you. God help me, I still love you."

At her words his whole body shuddered, and she was vaguely aware of a new tension in him as he lifted his head and stared into her eyes. Her fingers curled into his thick auburn hair, and she opened herself for him. Her beautiful face was soft with surrender.

He stared down at her hard, resisting the pressure of her hands trying to pull his face back to hers. The firelight was lambent in her brilliant eyes, her cheeks flushed, her soft body warmly aglow. He thought her loveliness utterly compelling. She was obviously willing, and the fire in his loins was almost unbearable. It was all he could do to stop, and his breath came in harsh, irregular gasps. But as Grant looked at the beautiful woman beneath him, her passionate words lingered in his mind, triggering feelings he'd thought were long dead. He knew from experience the danger of those feelings. Suddenly an agony of conflicting emotion gripped him, and he tore himself from her and rolled away, keeping his back to her.

"Love!" He groaned the word with painful anguish. "You've never known the meaning of that word!"

She curled her fingers tightly against her love-swollen lips to stifle her tiny cry of anguish. Her first sensations were that of loss and then shock. She stared at his broad, muscular back, glistening in the firelight like dark polished bronze. She was terribly aware of the coiled emotion in him. Slowly the intense pain of his rejection sank in and blotted out the glow of passion that had consumed her. For some reason he didn't want her. At the hurtful thought, she flushed scarlet with shame, and suddenly she was grateful that he wasn't looking at her. She'd practically thrown herself at him—at least that's what he must believe.

"Grant..." Even her soft voice trembled as she tried to reach out to him. "I didn't mean for this to

happen." The blankets rustled as she sat up. "I..."
She moved toward him.

He turned and his black gaze swept her lush
beauty. For an instant his male need almost overpowered his tight control. "For God's sake, cover
yourself," he rasped.

Hot crimson stained her cheeks as she became
aware of her nakedness and its effect on him. An
artist by nature, she'd never known a modest day in
her life except in moments like this, when someone
else made her acutely aware of her lack of modesty.

"I'm sorry," she said, deeply conscious of her
blunder. She was still blushing as she slowly drew
the blankets around her.

If anything she looked even sexier to him, partially covered, with her curved shoulders rising in
swanlike beauty above the garnet red wool. When
she adjusted the blankets, moving a tiny bit in his
direction, he growled, "Keep away from me." His
voice was taut and hard, his tone commanding.

Stung, and not comprehending that it was his intense desire for her and not disgust that caused him
to act thus, she shrank back against the blankets.
"What's wrong?"

"Eight damned years," he muttered savagely, "in
case you've forgotten."

"Of course I haven't. I couldn't, not ever," she

murmured, her pain as great as his. "But why did you kiss me tonight if you didn't want to?"

"Because I couldn't stop myself," he admitted, his rough voice full of self-loathing, his tone of self-hatred hurting her even more than his words. "You're the last woman I should have anything to do with—much less sleep with. Eight years ago you turned my life around so completely that I—"

"Turned *your* life around!" she whispered amazedly before sinking back into stunned silence as she remembered the terrible pain of his betrayal, of her teenage pregnancy, of the loss of the man she loved and of their baby and of her virtual imprisonment for the four years that had followed. What could he know of such misery, he who had cavalierly gone his way after what he must have considered an unimportant summer romance? In that moment, feeling all the old pain, she almost hated him. "After what you did to me, I shouldn't have anything to do with you." She broke off, overcome by emotions so intense she couldn't express them adequately with words. But the bitterness of her expression told him exactly how she was feeling.

"What I did to you!" His gruff words lashed her. "You were the one who lied to me, who led me on, and then when things got a little too serious, you ran home to Mama."

She stared at him blankly, determining that he

must have long ago rationalized his part in what had happened. He was the one who'd been after her money, who hadn't really wanted to make a commitment to her, who'd taken money from her mother and left her.

Memories that had been locked away for eight years whirled in her enraged mind, and they were startlingly vivid. She remembered the first night he'd made love to her as though it were only yesterday. The silver moon had shone in his black eyes as softly as the emotion she'd mistaken for intense love for her. Afterward he'd told her he wanted to marry her, that he couldn't live without her. She'd believed him when he said they would drive into Pittsburgh and tell their families together the next morning.

The memory of that night was as clear as if it were only yesterday. Her face had still been aglow from their lovemaking, her hair incriminatingly tumbled and adorned with wild columbine, stray leaves, moss and twigs from the ground when she let herself into Aunt Peggy's and tiptoed across the faded Oriental carpet in the grand salon toward her room. Suddenly Rosalind's voice had boomed out of nowhere, and then out of everywhere as it echoed in the vast house.

"Where have you been, Abigail? It's after three in the morning."

Startled, Abigail froze in mid-tiptoe, her state of dreamy euphoria instantly shattered.

"W-with Grant."

"Just what does that mean?"

"I'm going to marry him!"

"Really?" The voice moved nearer. "And who's Grant?" Rosalind switched on the great red Chinese lamp in the hall. Abigail squinted against the too-brilliant light and blushed, feeling terribly uncomfortable.

"Answer me!" Rosalind hissed in fury.

"He's from Pittsburgh, but he's from a poor family. You've never heard of his family."

"Doubtless he's poor, a fortune hunter, and quite unsuitable for you."

"He's poor, but he's not any of those other things!"

"Enough! I came to pick you up and drive you to see Aunt Gertie. She had a heart attack this afternoon and is in intensive care in Philadelphia."

"Oh, no!"

"Yes, darling. Waiting for you has delayed me hours getting to the hospital, but I couldn't leave without you, once I realized that what was going on right here was just as serious as Gertie's illness. I can't really do anything for her, but I can certainly do something about this."

"Mother, it's not what you think!"

"Then explain your wrinkled blouse, your tangled hair, your smudged lipstick. Need I go on? It's exactly what I think—probably worse!"

Abigail felt deeply shamed, but she managed stiffly, "I love him."

"Have the two of you been making love in the forest?"

Abigail went scarlet. "I don't have to answer that, Mother."

Rosalind's eyes widened with horror. "Then I know the answer!"

"He's going to marry me."

"Nonsense! I won't allow it. You're much too young for love and marriage. I've already packed your bags, Abigail. We're leaving this minute!"

"No! No! I can't go without telling him. I can't!"

Abigail had grown so distraught that Rosalind had ended by driving to Grant's cottage. But neither he, his things, or his car were there.

Rosalind had smiled in bitter triumph when Abigail came flying out of the empty house in tears.

"He's gone! Mother..."

"He certainly didn't waste any time."

"I don't understand."

"I'll explain everything, darling, on our way to Aunt Gertie's. It's one of the oldest and most predictable stories of all time, let me assure you."

Rosalind had explained with relish, and Abigail

had listened fearfully, only half believing her then. Later, when Grant didn't try to find her, she realized her authoritative mother was right.

Suddenly Abigail's mind cleared, and she was brought sharply back to the present—and to Grant, who was watching her with an anger every bit as fierce as her own. She was no longer a foolish, gullible teenager whom he could easily manipulate with a few sweet words and kisses. Apparently he'd twisted the facts to salve his own conscience.

Grant was staring at her hard, and she realized she had to say something, even though there was no profit in dredging up the past. More importantly she had to protect Michael.

"There were a lot of things you don't know," Abigail said evasively at last.

"There sure as hell were!" he muttered, staring at her hard, his black eyes intense and hostile. "But I see no reason to go into all that now."

"Good! I don't either."

It was a mutual standoff. They glared at one another, and the lengthening silence grew even more tense. Neither knew what to do or how to feel. There was an undeniable attraction between them as well as a deep anger. Abigail did feel a certain grudging gratitude toward him for having prevented their making love, though it piqued her feminine vanity and her Bainbridge pride that she hadn't been the one to stop him.

Suddenly she realized how utterly stupid she'd been to have come to Grant's cabin for help at such an hour. She should have realized something like this might happen.

Her mind searched frantically for a suitable alternative to her predicament. She could have parked in front of her aunt's gate and slept in the car until daylight, and then she could have driven back to the nearest farmhouse and asked for help. But the thought simply hadn't occurred to her, and now that it did, it certainly held no appeal.

A bolt of lightning flashed, its brilliance illuminating every window. The whole cottage seemed to shudder. Even now she had no desire to go out in that storm and sleep in her car. Still, she wished she were a million miles from this virile man who continued to stare at her with such relentless interest. She might as well get dressed, use his phone and leave, she thought drearily at last.

At just that moment her stomach, aware only of its own need and oblivious to the emotionally charged atmosphere, grumbled so raucously that even he heard it. They were both instantly reminded that because of their passionate activity she hadn't eaten, and suddenly he smiled at her, the tension lessening visibly.

Her mind returned longingly to her untouched supper in the kitchen. When she thought of the heaped potatoes and gravy and the steaming roast she'd so carelessly abandoned and subsequently forgotten when he'd kissed her, her mouth almost watered. That she could have failed to eat when she was so hungry said volumes for his sex appeal. She stared up at him in irritation. In her present mood, no hunk of virility, no matter how toe-curling, was worth that sacrifice. It was with deep regret that she thought of going the rest of the night without eating. Nevertheless, she decided dismally, she really had no choice. Wearily, she leaned forward and reached for her clothes.

Anticipating her intention, he stunned her by scooping up her wet clothes himself and holding the soggy bundle out of her reach. "Not so fast." His tone was deceptively mild, and at her startled expression, he drawled, "I guess our passionate reunion was as good a way as any of persuading you to get out of these clothes before you come down with pneumonia, and I certainly don't intend to let you get back into them now." He was smiling casually, as though he hadn't said or done anything out of the ordinary, as though those weren't her clothes, and she wasn't naked beneath his blanket.

She found his calm maddening when her own

thoughts were still a whirl of turmoil. "Give me my clothes!"

He held onto the sodden mess as though it were a highly prized treasure. "You won't need them until the morning."

"What?"

"There's a little something I neglected to tell you earlier," his low voice continued as she stared at him in growing irritation.

His phrase, "a little something I neglected to tell you," rang ominously in her mind, and she had a very distinct sinking feeling that she really didn't want to hear what he was going to say next.

He drawled off-handedly, "The phone went out about a half an hour before you drove up. You won't be calling your aunt tonight—or anyone else for that matter. It's either sleep here with me or in your car, and being the gallant gentleman that I am—"

"Your phone went out, and you didn't tell me?"

He nodded. "If I admit I was insatiably curious when I saw the grand Abigail Bainbridge on my doorstep without her designer mop, will you forgive me for omitting that…er…rather pertinent fact?" He paused as though politely waiting for her reply. When there was none, he went on. "And now—" Thunder rumbled violently through the forest, and he was forced to pause a second time. In the ensuing silence he continued, ''Being the gentleman that I am, I can't send you out in that.''

There was a quality in his voice that baited her, but she refused to be drawn, even though her mind recoiled at the word *gentleman* and the tone with which he said it.

''I wouldn't presume to intrude further on your evening,'' she said stiffly, thinking glumly of a long cramped night in her Volkswagen and the cheerless prospect of having only her grumbling stomach for company.

''Oh, but I insist that you do intrude further. So far it's been most...'' His dark eyes flashed with amusement. ''...most interesting.''

''I have no intention of spending the night with you!'' She bristled.

''Maybe not, but you will,'' he murmured dryly, his lips quirking into a devastatingly white smile. ''If there's one thing growing up with five sisters taught me, it's that females, especially those with ladylike airs, put a much higher value on creature comforts than men. I can't imagine you out in the dark in that storm, huddled and shivering in your wet clothes in that tin rattletrap of yours, when I'm willing to share my own bed—one which I can highly recommend.''

This last statement, pregnant with sexual innuendo, sent warm shivers through her. Defiantly she lifted her face and met his gaze as though his words had had no effect. With an effort, he swallowed a chuckle.

"How absolutely princely of you," she fumed. "But I couldn't possibly put you out of it."

"You're stretching my gallantry a bit, sweet," he said, his voice huskily mocking. "I never said anything about myself being put out of it. There's more than enough room for two."

"Of course! Knowing you, I should have realized that was what you had in mind," she snapped, furious again at allowing herself to be drawn further into his impossible conversation. "I really would prefer my car." Her voice sounded strangely weak, not nearly as coldly rejecting as she wanted it. But she found it absurdly difficult not to imagine herself cozily ensconced in his warm, snug bed, wrapped in the delicious warmth of his arms. Even as she thought of it, a treacherous golden fire heated her arteries.

"Then you're the only woman in three counties who would make such a noble sacrifice," he taunted.

She was reminded that most women were very attracted to his dark virile good looks and knew he was well aware of that fact. In the past Grant and she had frequently joked about it. "I could write a book about what it's like to be thought of as a mere sex object for the opposite sex when my own fond interest in them is strictly brotherly," he'd teased her on more than one occasion. "Don't bother," she'd returned, "most people wouldn't have much sympathy."

She probably was the only woman in three counties who wouldn't jump at his invitation, but then she was probably far more vulnerable where he was concerned than those other women.

"Let me assure you it's no sacrifice," she said, again forcing coldness into her tone.

"I find that rather difficult to believe. A while ago you acted as though you hadn't had a man in eight years!" His smile was as smooth as his voice.

She turned white with rage. The barb cut, for it was too close to the truth.

"Weren't you expecting someone else when I drove up?" she asked.

"Yes." His keen, observant stare seemed to go right through her. "Are you jealous?"

"No!" she howled, but that wasn't altogether true. A sudden heat stained her cheeks with deep color, and she fervently hoped that she hadn't given him the satisfaction of seeing her instantly burn with jealousy. "Then, I really should be going," Abigail said too hastily, momentarily in the grip of feelings that only made her all the more angry at herself and him.

"I don't think she'll be coming in this weather," he replied, uncaringly emphasizing that it had been a woman he was expecting. "While she has an undeniable weakness for my rugged brand of charm—" his eyes were flashing with the most annoying amusement, and Abigail realized he was enjoying himself immensely "—I'm hardly so conceited to think she can't live without me for one night. Women are like soft and very sensible cats. There are few tidbits worth going out in a rain like this for, even one as delectable as myself."

"Please spare me your obnoxious conceit and your rather infantile philosophizing."

"Chauvinistic," he corrected helpfully. "And if she does, she'd hardly stay…since you're here. Surely you haven't forgotten I'm a one-woman man! And right now, you're woman enough for me."

"I won't be here!" Abigail snapped, clutching the blanket about her as she started to get up.

"The hell you won't!" His tone was low, but she caught the new element of command in it, his teasing mood having changed abruptly into one strongly charged with the deepest emotion.

His urgent passion electrified her. The emotional climate was instantly changed.

"You wouldn't keep me here against my will?" she asked softly, a tiny, thrilling fear coursing through her in spite of herself. For all that it was the twentieth century, there had always been something deliciously uncivilized about him. He belonged to another age. For an instant she imagined him a proud buccaneer and herself a comely maiden he intended to ravish, and the thought was not nearly as unappealing as she would have liked.

He read the expression on her flushed face with amazing accuracy. "Don't be so melodramatic," he stated baldly. "You're staying, and there's an end to it. You walked back into my life tonight, and you're not walking out until I'm damn well ready."

The fear went out of her face, as well as that indefinable expression of anticipation he found alluring.

"I guess I'd better find you something dry to put on," he said, forcing his gaze from the tantalizing curve of breasts that rose above the blanket she was clasping. He wondered if she had any idea how she affected him. He rose and purposefully strode toward his bedroom, trying in vain to erase the provocative vision of golden flesh mysteriously veiled in scarlet wool. "Something bulky I can't see through so that the sight of you doesn't drive me crazy," he muttered almost savagely.

"All right," she agreed meekly, shamelessly pleased at his admission of how deeply she affected him. The other woman no longer seemed so important, and the jealous feeling was rapidly fading.

He returned almost at once and threw her a large plaid flannel shirt. ''I hope that comes to your ankles! When you get dressed, go back into the kitchen and finish eating. If you can't figure out how to use the microwave, call me. I'll be in the bedroom watching television. There's a good late movie that started a little while ago.''

In a flash she recalled his penchant for late movies when he had trouble sleeping. In the past they'd often watched them together, popping popcorn and cuddling. With an effort she pushed the pleasant memories from her mind, but not before he noted the softening in her face.

He was whistling as he walked from the room, but she was more sharply aware than ever of the danger of him.

Four

The red blanket slid to the floor, revealing golden skin and alluring female curves. A tangle of tawny hair streamed down Abigail's slender back as she reached for the blue plaid shirt Grant had thrown her. As she slipped into it, she was sensually aware of his scent clinging to it, of the softness of the fabric caressing her skin. Like a high school girl, she experienced a strange thrill to be wearing an item of Grant's apparel, and she felt very small and feminine in his shirt.

His garment swallowed her. The shoulder seams practically fell to her elbows, causing her to imagine the breadth of Grant's shoulders; the hem brushed beneath her knees. She nervously rolled up the sleeves, then buttoned the front of the shirt.

The cottage was so cozy and small that it wasn't possible to share it with Grant without being conscious of him. She was very aware of every sound coming from the bedroom—the noise of the television, the occasional burst of his rich, musical laughter, the sound of water splashing in the bathroom lavatory during a commercial, the creak of the mattress as Grant shifted his weight. Nor could she escape the appeal of a certain recurring mental vision—that of the negligent, masculine sprawl of his length upon the tumbled covers of his king-size bed while the other side of his bed remained invitingly vacant.

She had no business being here—like this—with him. What was she going to do? When she'd left Pittsburgh intending to confront Grant, she'd never expected anything like this to happen. And she was totally unprepared to deal with this virile, charismatic man who still compelled her with the same intensity he had all those years ago. She'd allowed him to kiss her, to undress her, even to seduce her—though fortunately he'd stopped himself in time.

Remembering those torrid moments, her flesh grew hot, and her black-fringed eyelids drowsily descended to shutter the feverish sparkle of her iridescent blue eyes. With a quick indrawn breath, her sense of reality drifted away, and once again she experienced the too-pleasant, shivering thrill of his hands gliding intimately over her body, his lightest touch erotically disturbing her. Dreamy, she remembered the wondrous sensation of his lips brushing the moist velvet texture of hers, of his tongue exploring the soft, sensual outline of her mouth before his kiss had deepened into complete possession. She could almost feel the hardness of his body pressing against hers, his heated flesh warming her like a raw blaze, his muscular strength wrapping her tightly so that she was aware only of him, only of his body next to her own open softness, only of his masculinity and taut male need for her. How damp and erotically hot she'd felt then, how totally willing to surrender herself to those wonderful feelings, to him. It had been a moment of wanton magic that swept away the years of desolation and pain spent without a man's love—without his love, for Grant was the only man she'd ever loved. All of her sexual coldness had melted with that one blazing kiss, and she'd felt like a woman again. She thought of spring blossoms unfolding in riotous, glorious beauty after long, barren months of winter. Though she and Grant hadn't consummated their love, she'd known that she still irrevocably belonged to him.

Like Sleeping Beauty, one kiss had awakened all of the old yearnings and passions that Abigail had fought so hard to deny. But now she could see the truth more clearly than she desired to. In spite of everything, she wanted him still. But she knew this was not a fairy-tale world, and he was no charming prince who could make her happily-ever-after fantasy come true. She was a Bainbridge, and he could never belong in her world.

With the deliberateness of a quick slap, she swung herself instantly into a standing position, forcing her thoughts away from the passion Grant had so easily stirred, away from a terrible longing that could never be assuaged. Her heart ached. She knew too well the man he was, and he deserved no love from her.

Feet bare, she scampered lightly across the cold stone floor to the kitchen, but she scarcely noticed the coldness. She wished she could escape all the feelings threatening to destroy her.

She slammed about the kitchen in frustration. If only she could put Grant and all that he meant to her out of her mind. While she reheated her plate of food in the microwave, her dismal thoughts remained focused on him. She went to the refrigerator and poured herself a glass of milk. Then the timer went off, and she sat down to eat. She was scarcely conscious of eating, of anything other than her depression.

Within minutes she'd consumed everything and sat staring at her empty plate. Though she felt replete, physically content and suddenly very sleepy, she remained incapable of putting Grant from her thoughts. When she inadvertently envisioned him in his bedroom, a treacherous part of her felt the longing to join him and curl intimately beside his warm masculine body on the softness of his bed.

In vain she attempted to dismiss the pleasant image. She should try to exorcise his hold over her, not surrender to it like some love-starved fool. She stood up, intending to go to the sink and wash the dishes.

The husky resonance of an all-too-familiar masculine tone filled the kitchen, vibrating through her, causing a vague shivery sensation to spread throughout her body.

"Abigail…"

Grant didn't even have to touch her. His mere voice was like a physical caress.

Abigail's fingers fumbled with the dishes. A renewed fury pulsated through her because of her treacherous response.

"Leave them," Grant said from the doorway.

Abigail whirled and was startled to see that he had discarded his blue cotton shirt and now was wearing a navy velour robe that revealed a wide V of bronzed, male skin. Her pulse fluctuated wildly in alarm, and she was aware of a vague sensation of danger. No smile softened the slashing line of his mouth. She tore her gaze from the rippling muscles of his chest and torso, from the black curling hairs that faintly covered his body, but not before the female part of her sensed the latent power in his physique. She thought he made a deliberate effort to restrain some ancient, masculine instinct as his avid black eyes swept her.

A savage gust of wind battered the cottage, rattling the windowpanes. A tree limb crashed to the ground outside. Abigail was terribly conscious of the vast darkness of the woods outside, of the violence of the storm, of the isolation of the cottage. She was very much alone with this tall dark man, and a strange, sexual tension seemed to fill the tiny room.

Grant had come into the kitchen for a beer, but the sight of her looking so fragile and lovely in his shirt sent his pulse racing violently. The beer was instantly forgotten. Hell, she looked good in anything. His rough masculine work shirt only intensified her feminine sexuality instead of diminishing it. And Grant was more forcibly aware than ever of his male vulnerability to her soft female allure.

His gaze raked appraisingly downward from her startled, too-blue eyes, their vivid color enhanced by the deep blue of his shirt, to her moist lips, the pale curve of her graceful neck and her full breasts that jutted temptingly against the soft fabric of his shirt. Long, shapely legs, golden in color, brought it sharply to his mind that she was naked beneath his shirt. The fire in his loins made him want to rip the shirt from her body and pull her into his arms, but he fought the impulse. Nevertheless, the tumbling profusion of her silky hair made him recall other times when her hair had looked thus, after he'd made love to her.

"I...I...don't mind," she whispered, totally unaware of her power over him.

"Mind what?" He'd become so engrossed in her sensual allure that he'd lost the thread of their conversation.

"Washing dishes," she murmured, turning away from him and toward the sink as if to do so.

If she hadn't turned away, he might have been able to resist going near her. But the male in him wanted her attention focused on him instead of on the dishes.

He was beside her at once, hesitating for a long moment, restraining hands that longed to touch her. She was deeply conscious of him. Through the material of the shirt she wore she could almost feel the heat of his flat stomach graze her back as he reached around her with his arms, forcing her against the counter, his great body enveloping hers, touching hers, firing her blood with sweet excited rapture. In a daze of confusion, she set the dishes down on the counter with a clatter.

"And I thought I was a more conscientious housekeeper than you," he whispered teasingly, his warm breath fanning her damp hair. "I never wash dishes at midnight." Her sweet, feminine scent drifted to his nostrils, and he inhaled deeply.

She felt the pressure of his chin as he gently rested it on the top of her head for a moment. "You are...better than I," she admitted breathlessly, treacherously conscious of him as a man, of the urgency of his male response to her. "You know I've never been very good at keeping house," she continued shyly. She tilted her lovely face and stared up at him through the sweep of dark lashes. From the corner of her eye she fleetingly glimpsed the swarthiness of his rough cheek and the waving, burnished darkness of his hair.

His arms slid around her so that his hands could cup the fullness of her breasts. "I know," he said as though he really didn't care whether she kept house or not. He lifted a handful of her hair so that his lips could brush against the sensitive flesh at the base of her neck.

"I suppose it's because housework..." she began falteringly, trying unsuccessfully to ignore the tiny sensual ripples running through her as his fingers gently rubbed her nipples to taut erection. Everywhere his body touched hers she felt aflame.

"You're not inspired in that department,' he suggested quietly, his lips pressing into her hair. His hands were unbuttoning her shirt so they could slide inside and explore the warm satiny flesh beneath. "Besides, you grew up in a house with servants, and you never had to learn how to take care of yourself properly."

"Perhaps," she admitted, not really thinking of what he was saying but of the delicious sensations he was evoking as his roaming hands slid over her velvety skin.

"And I had five sisters to teach me how to do things," he murmured absently. "Keeping house is only a matter of good habits. I can easily teach you—as they taught me. But right now I can think of other, far more interesting things to teach you."

"It makes me feel inadequate as a woman not to be able to do—"

"Shh!" he admonished huskily. "You should never feel inadequate as a woman."

His grip shifted, and she felt his hands clasp her shoulders, hard and demanding as he turned her in his arms.

His dark eyes stared deeply into hers. "I was a fool to come back and demand to see you," he said at last, feeling himself inexorably drawn by her exquisite golden beauty. "But you see, I've never been able to forget you."

"Nor I you," she murmured as his lips descended

to claim hers in the lightest and most tender of kisses. Deliberately he restrained the hot tide of passion that swept him the instant his mouth touched hers and he felt her body melt against his.

Not trusting himself to kiss her again, he pulled back and regarded her for a long silent moment. "Things always get out of hand between you and me," he said at last. The huskiness of his voice wrapped her with its velvet sensuality.

"They always did," she murmured dreamily, wishing he would go on kissing her and holding her, though she realized how foolish that would be.

"Yes," he said slowly, thinking her unutterably lovely as he remembered the flaming passion of their love all those years ago.

Her hands moved to his and she laced her fingers through his, removing them from her body. "Perhaps this time we should try…to be more careful," she suggested hesitantly. Her sapphire eyes were luminous in her beautiful face, and he could not resist their mute appeal.

"Yes, I suppose we should," he admitted reluctantly, smiling down at her. "Why don't you come watch the movie with me?"

"Are you sure that's wise—I mean, that that's all you have in mind?" she asked.

His eyes swept over the exposed curves of her lush breasts swelling provocatively against his chest.

"It's not all I have in mind," he admitted, "but it's all we'll do. Scout's honor." He affected a boyish grin that was charmingly at variance with his mature, masculine features.

"You were never a Scout a day in your life," she chided softly.

"You know me too well. But my sisters were Girl Scouts, if that counts." He chuckled, his boyish grin returning to devastate her senses a second time. He removed his hand from hers and brought it to her breast again.

"Grant…" she began falteringly, not understanding.

"I was only going to button your shirt," he returned gallantly. "It needs doing rather badly, if I'm to cling to my…er…Scout's honor." She felt a sensation like an electric shock as his fingers accidentally grazed her flesh.

She jumped back. "Perhaps it would be safer if I did that myself."

"Perhaps," he returned with lazy reluctance, leaving her to complete the task as he went to the refrigerator to get a beer. "Want one?" he drawled.

"All right," she murmured.

Already he was popping the top of a second beer and wrapping the frosty can in a napkin for her.

"Come on then," he said. "The commercial's

probably over, and we're missing part of the movie.''

''What are you watching?'' she asked as he led her toward the bedroom. She was keenly aware of his fingers lightly touching the back of her waist.

''It Happened One Night,'' he returned easily. ''It's one of my favorite old Clark Gable films. I've seen it several times before. It's about a rich girl who's engaged to marry the wrong man. She doesn't care a whit for him and spends most of the movie traveling around the country with Clark Gable and sleeping in a certain motel with him. Gable's very noble, of course, and hangs a blanket between their beds.''

''Sounds very suggestive.'' Abigail smiled up at him as she realized his gaze was fastened on her.

''For its time, it was,'' he agreed as he led her through the living room.

''Does she...?'' Abigail was suddenly pensive, and the question lodged in her throat like a large painful lump.

''Does she what?''

''Marry the wrong man?''

''Are you kidding?'' He grinned broadly down at her, his expression superior. ''That's what I like about movies. Everything always comes out right in the end; the good guy always gets the girl.'' He was staring at Abigail, and his expression was oddly intense. "She marries Clark Gable, of course," he said at last. His eyes moved leisurely over Abigail's delicate features, pausing on her soft, rose lips.

"Of course," she murmured, feeling dazed from the warm emotion he was arousing with his lingering gaze.

They stepped into his bedroom, vaguely aware of the sound and the bluish-gray glare of the television in one corner. Grant drew her down onto the bed beside him. When she started to move to the farthest edge of the mattress, he pulled her relentlessly to him.

"There's no point in trying to avoid me," he said knowingly, "when I mean to keep you near me." He was teasing her, and his devilishly wicked grin lent a roguish charm to his handsome features. "Besides, it's what you want, too, and your character is equally as weak as mine when it comes to resisting temptation." There was a glowing intensity in his jet-black eyes that sent a wave of hot color into her cheeks.

"I can too resist temptation," she snapped, not at all sure that she could as she tried to draw away. Still, it displeased her that he considered her so easy.

"I won't argue the point," he murmured lightly, without relinquishing the small wrist in his own hard grip, "if you insist on taking it as a slight to your womanly virtue. But as I see it, you're just a girl with a bit of common sense. Why should you try to resist temptation, when not resisting it is so much more fun?'' He regarded her shapely figure with admiration, and what he saw stirred him considerably more than he allowed his bland, teasing tone to reveal. ''I've never understood why we are supposed to fervently believe that self-denial is so virtuous.'' The smile in his voice reminded her that he was remembering how wantonly responsive she'd once been with him. ''You're passionate and warm and...everything a man wants in bed.''

Again a strange warmth suffused her pale skin. ''I...I'm not like that with everyone.''

''I wouldn't have you any other way,'' he countered gently, smiling down at her. ''I like wild women. Most men do.''

Wild women! Generations of Bainbridges would have hopelessly entangled themselves in their shrouds as they twisted in moldy crypts had they heard one of their own assigned to such a category.

''I don't find your use of plurals particularly flattering,'' she grumbled.

''I was trying to be truthful, not flattering,'' he returned absently. At her darkening scowl his voice became falsely solicitous. ''Jealous?'' One of his dark eyebrows quirked wickedly in her direction.

''Of course not!'' she declared in new fury.

''Maybe I don't find that answer of yours particularly flattering," he returned, a broad, infuriating grin on his face as he repeated her turn of phrase.

"I wouldn't intentionally flatter you, you big dope! Your ego's already as bloated as a dead toad!"

He chuckled good-naturedly at her outburst and plumped a pillow. Then stretching negligently so that the hard muscles of his thighs flexed beneath his tight-fitting jeans and robe, he leaned against the clump of pillows next to the brass headboard. She was huffily edging away from him when he reached out and pulled her to him, settling her against himself. When he did so, his robe fell open, revealing a discomfiting expanse of brown shoulders and broad, furred chest.

She was fuming, but now that the commercials were over, he was thankful she was disposed, at least for the moment, to fume in silence.

His great arm moved absently beneath the damp, spilling golden mass of her hair. She was intensely aware of his nearness, of the growing warmth their touching bodies generated. The intimacy of sharing his bed with him was almost more than her shattered nerves could endure.

He was infuriating! Deliberately so! She lay in silence, unable to think of anything further to say— not that he would have listened. Grant was watching the movie avidly, as though he'd never seen it before, and for a time she too became caught up in the story. Unlike him she wasn't a night owl. She sipped her beer slowly, and as she lay wrapped in the luxurious warmth of Grant's arms, her head resting on his shoulder, a deep contentment stole over her, and she fell sound asleep. She wasn't aware of him leaving her to switch off the television much later or of him opening the window so that he could hear the sound of the rain pattering outside while he lay with her nestled in his arms. Nor did she know that he stripped to the buff before he slid into bed beside her and lightly caressed her, smoothing back her hair and tucking the covers tightly about her.

Grant lay in the darkness for a long time, unable to sleep. He was too deeply conscious of the woman whose warm body lay wound in an intimate knot with his.

His expression was grim, his features so rigid they seemed hewn of coppery stone. Gone was the man of easy smiles. A volcanic fury churned within him.

Abigail sighed with the contentment of one whose dreams were sweetly voluptuous, and one of her silken arms wrapped around his chest. He felt the lightness of her, the warmth of her in his arms. The air was scented with her haunting fragrance.

Her sweetness was driving him crazy! He wanted to hate her, but he couldn't. He looked down at her face. Her skin was so smooth it felt like warm satin.

He brushed her brow tenderly with his palm. In sleep she looked young and vulnerable, not the pretentious snob she wanted to be. She aroused odd, misplaced protective feelings in him. Her other hand roamed lightly beneath the sheets, tracing the shape of his maleness. He caught his breath sharply and lay very still beneath her exploring fingertips.

His pulse quickened from her wanton massage, and he grew aware of a potent desire to pull her beneath him and possess her with the passionate hunger of a savage taking what was his.

Instead of giving into the violence of his passions, he gently unclasped her fingers from his silken-tipped masculinity and pushed her hand away. She moaned, knowing little of the turmoil she aroused. He forced himself to remember a certain photograph he'd seen in the Pittsburgh newspaper of a most sanctimonious and unpleasant-looking individual. The article had described Harold Harrison as the most eligible bachelor in Pennsylvania. Grant frowned at the memory, because every time he thought of Harrison, he visualized Abigail in Harrison's arms. It rankled Grant that he couldn't compete against Harrison and what he could give her. No matter how much Grant wanted her, Abigail was not his, and she never had been or could be, except during a few stolen moments.

Grant actually believed that Abigail had been

right when she'd left him eight years ago and that he had been wrong to blame her for it. But her leaving had hurt like hell despite that, and he hadn't ever forgiven her.

She belonged to a glittery, phony world in which he could never fit. After she'd left him, he'd thought that he could work to become the kind of man her mother wouldn't reject. He'd found in the end he hadn't wanted to succeed at that, not even for Abigail. That left too little room for individuality.

Soon Abigail would be married to this scion of her world. She'd take her place as a reigning queen. Grant had made decisions about what to do with his life, and they couldn't include her. But that did not stop him from wanting her as keenly as he ever had. Still, tomorrow he would leave her. Just as there was no place for him in her world, there was no place for her in the life he had deliberately chosen.

He despised himself for still wanting anything from this woman-child who'd betrayed him eight years ago. Why did he have to prove to her that he wasn't completely wrong for her? But he did, and before he was through, he was determined that she would suffer with this knowledge exactly as he had. Was this but a subtle brand of revenge?

The desire of revenge was not usually his style. He should have forgotten her long ago and found someone else. But always when he'd tried, he'd found himself measuring each new relationship against the perfection of the three months he'd spent with her. He had never wanted another woman as he wanted her. Eight years ago, his passion for her had nearly consumed him with pain. Now it was her turn to ache for him when he left.

In her sleep she murmured his name, and a strange kind of longing overcame him as she nestled herself against him. Everywhere her body touched his, his skin burned as though touched by a raw flame.

He was a soft, stupid fool where she was concerned. That was his last angry thought before he too fell asleep in her arms.

Five

Golden sunlight streamed through the windows, bathing the man and woman who lay together, their bodies warmly touching, their limbs and arms intertwining as though they had just made wild, passionate love. Outside, all was hushed and still and brilliant after the violence of the storm.

A dewy moisture glistened on the crimson orange blaze of maple and birch leaves. Near the house a small peach orchard and garden had been carved out of the forest, and enormous pumpkins gleamed like great golden balls amidst a brown field of stubble. Beyond the wind whispered through the dried tassels of swaying cornstalks.

A fresh, woodsy scent sifted through one partially opened window. Abigail's lashes fluttered drowsily open to the sound of a squirrel scampering about, rustling the thick carpet of leaves and brown stubble.

Inadvertently, Abigail's gaze wandered to where her slender hands rested on Grant's body. Her left hand lay lightly upon the warmth of his dark, furred chest. No diamond flashed from her ring finger; there was no evidence of her promise to another man. Rosalind and Harold had agreed it was much wiser to leave the extremely valuable Harrison diamond locked safely away in a safety deposit box. Abigail, who thought jewelry a nuisance, had been happy not to have to wear the ornate engagement ring.

As she lay in Grant's arms, nestled against him with a complete sense of belonging only to him, it seemed impossible that she could ever be a wife to any other man.

Had her one too-passionate love ruined her for another man's love? Could she make her marriage work? But she had to try. She had Michael to think of. He needed a father, and she had longed for the chance to mother him. The years were slipping by, and she didn't have many more to spend with her little boy.

For the first time she wondered about Grant and what he'd done with his life in the past eight years.

He'd made no mention of a career, of his work. The cottage, though neat and clean, was far from luxurious. Indeed, it was as rough and masculine as ever. Had he become a doctor? Or had he given up on that?

Abigail could not marry a man who wasn't capable of giving her independence apart from her family. He didn't have to be rich. With marriage she hoped gradually to escape her mother's power. If she married a man who couldn't support her, that would never be possible.

She realized suddenly that her thoughts were wandering in a ridiculous maze, since eight years ago Grant hadn't wanted to marry her. He'd wanted her physically with all the youthful desperation of male need, but when his feelings had been put to the test, he'd proven he hadn't felt real love. Even his discovery that she was pregnant hadn't changed his mind, and that was absolute proof there had been no depth to the passion he'd felt for her.

Grant stirred, awakening. Abigail's fresh, female scent assailed his nostrils. He felt her soft body enmeshed with his, and at first he thought that he was still dreaming. The tumbling mass of her gold hair spilled over onto his own pillow. As he shook off his drowsiness, he realized that living, warm feminine flesh lay pressed closely to him. He reached for her, burying his sensual lips against the white curve of her throat and kissing her. The unexpected heat of his lips sent a rush of wildfire through her arteries. She moaned until his low chuckle of delight brought her to her senses, and she fought to wrench herself away from him.

"Not so fast, sweet," he murmured with a smile, dragging her beneath his hard, masculine body so that she was very aware of his aroused manliness. He grinned down at her. "Why do you pretend that you're unwilling?"

She met the frank appraisal in his eyes.

"Because I should be," she admitted truthfully. "I haven't seen you for eight years, and I… shouldn't feel…"

"I know." He smoothed a wayward tendril of gold from her face.

"You see, I thought I was over you," she said softly, letting her eyes wander over the handsome and pleasantly smiling features of the man who'd haunted her for eight years. The sensation of his hand in her hair was treacherously pleasant.

"So did I. I told myself you were fat and ugly and the mother of three sniffling kids—I guess because I knew if I didn't think of you like that, I'd go crazy and might have to see you again,' he returned huskily. He twined the golden strand he was holding about his finger and brought it to his lips to kiss its sweet fragrance. "And that was exactly what happened when I saw your engagement picture in the Pittsburgh paper. Even though I knew I shouldn't have anything to do with you, I was determined to see you—one last time.'' The faintest trace of bitterness in his deep tone gave emphasis to his last three words.

"One last time…" The phrase echoed ominously in her mind.

"You see, Abbie," he continued, "I've never had a shred of willpower where you're concerned. You're all wrong for me. I know that. You're a narcotic, and I'm an addict. I want to reform, but like too many addicts, no matter how hard I try, I can't get the initial sweetness of the drug out of my mind. When I'm weak—like now when the drug is temptingly available—I want to play around with it again, even though I realize its potential to destroy me." He bent his head hungrily to hers, this time seeking her lips.

"Is that what you're doing—playing around with me?"

"Not exactly."

His answer was cryptic, but his tone was strangely grim. She felt increasingly uneasy as his mouth nibbled lightly at her chin and began to wander in a flaming path toward her lips.

Despite the pleasant sensations his kisses evoked,

she was too disturbed by the drift of his conversation to enjoy them.

"Grant, I want to talk to you."

"Well, I don't—not when there's something else I'd much rather be doing."

In vain she attempted to twist her face to avoid his, but her every movement only brought her more sharply aware of his powerful thighs against her legs, of his great, hard body on top of hers. The fact that she sought to evade his kiss merely spiced his interest.

With an easiness that infuriated her, he caught her chin in his warm brown fingers. Her blue eyes sparked with fire as she stared up into the smiling handsomeness of his face, then his mouth closed over hers in a deeply intimate kiss.

His mouth moved over hers fiercely, hungrily, forcing her lips open. His tongue played along the edges of swollen softness before slipping inside to taste her inner sweetness. All of her resistance crumbled beneath the gentle onslaught of his mouth. His hands slid downward, beneath the shirt she wore, which had twisted above her waist. Easily he molded her feminine shape to himself.

Desire as hot and scalding as liquid fire burned through her, threatening to consume her. Weakly she pushed against him, and when he removed his lips from hers so that he could seek out the sensitive flesh beneath her earlobe before he trailed hot scorching kisses down her neck, she whispered frantically, "Grant…stop…please! We…can't!" Yet even as she protested, tiny shudders of ecstasy rippled through her.

"Why not?" he murmured distractedly, lowering his mouth to nibble the delicate temptations of her rosy, erect nipples.

He knew too much about women and the erogenous parts of their anatomies, and he was using all his expertise to tantalize her. He was deliberately setting her aflame with a feverish need of him.

His lips gorged upon the feminine mounds of flesh. He sucked and nibbled on their spongy roseate tips; he nuzzled the swelling softness of her, exploring every contour of her womanly shape. At last he lovingly and triumphantly kissed the violent drumbeat beneath her left breast.

She felt his hand move intimately between her thighs to tease her with caresses.

He knew exactly what he was doing just as he knew how thoroughly he aroused her!

Tiny thrilling spasms erupted in her belly. They were the rumbling beginnings of a terrible, agonized hunger for him. It was as though she'd been slowly starving for him for eight years, and now her need was a rampaging force she couldn't control.

She pushed against his head, trying to remove her

breasts from his feasting lips before it was too late. But he caught her hands in one of his and held them tightly above her head against the cool metal of the brass headboard. She was his captive maiden and he the bold buccaneer determined to continue the insolent, ravaging onslaught that inflamed every female sense in her being.

She was aching with frustration, and the agony of her need was in her voice when she pleaded, "Oh, Grant, please…please…"

He lifted his mouth from her tingling flesh. "Are you begging me to stop or go on?" his deep, vibrant voice teased.

Her love-swollen breasts felt moist and warm from his kisses as the cool air swept over them.

"To…to…"

He grinned at her obvious state of indecision. She closed her eyes. It was difficult to lie, and even more difficult when she had to look at him.

He wasn't looking at her face, but at her heaving, love-dampened breasts.

Only with the greatest effort could she say the words that denied the truest emotion in her heart and the deepest need of her body. "To…stop," she whispered at last.

His low, velvet chuckle caressed her, but he did not draw away.

He lowered his head and continued to kiss her

breasts and her throat. He licked the shadowy dimple of her navel until she lay gasping, awash in desire and golden emotion as rivulets of sensation radiated from her belly.

"Why don't we get up," she began weakly. "I'll make breakfast, and we can have a long talk and decide what we're going to do."

She had dared to open her eyes again, and she stared down at his dark head pressed against her stomach. His hot tongue was curving in and out of the moist crevice, and she felt crazily breathless with the effects of it.

At last he looked up and tossed her one of his easy, white smiles. "But I already know what we're going to do, sweet," he said evenly. "I'm going to have a long leisurely breakfast in bed—you," he murmured. "For the first course, I'm going to kiss you here." He raised his lips to nibble the hot flesh at her throat. "Hmmm. Every part of you is as delicious as a honeyed roll, though some parts are more tartly delicious than others." He licked at her soft skin. "You're hot, too."

Beneath his ravaging mouth, her heart pounded like a wild pagan song filled with primeval passions and desire.

Denying her feelings, she tried to twist away, but he held her in a grip as strong as steel. Her soft breasts were ground against the coarse hairs of his muscled chest; the voluptuous softness of her hips against his thighs.

He deliberately forced her slender body into more intimate contact with his hard maleness. His leg slid between her legs, parting them as he eased himself over her. The blue shirt that she was wearing had twisted beneath her arms so that every part of her bared body was exposed to him. The thrusting tips of her breasts pressed intimately against his chest; her long legs were aligned with his.

She felt his male flesh sliding erotically against her.

"S-stop…"

"You know as well as I, it's far too late to stop," he murmured.

She gasped, and his husky chuckle enveloped her. A mist of sweat moistened both their bodies.

His mouth moved downward.

"And for the second course, your lips."

"Grant…"

Her hair was a shower of spilling gold as she turned her face away from his.

"Don't fight me, Abbie. It's no use. It's a battle we've both fought and lost, or we wouldn't be like this right now."

As his mouth moved toward hers she cried out, "Don't! Please!"

He laughed down at her, enjoying her dramatic

gesture and her obvious powerlessness against his superior strength and determination. She was protesting verbally, but her body was arched in wanton eagerness to accept his. Her tongue had erotically moistened her mouth in anticipation of his lips.

She offered one last argument. "Grant, don't do this." Scarcely about to think, she seized the first cliché that flitted through her mind. "Sexual passion without understanding doesn't mean anything!"

His expression hardened. His mouth hovered an inch above hers.

"Baby, you don't have to tell me that! That's one lesson I learned the hard way, and you were the one who taught it to me. Remember? You gave me everything in bed, and I found out it meant nothing to you. Unfortunately I lost my soul in the process, and that, my love, was very very painful. Even now after eight years—I haven't fully recovered."

"I don't know what you mean."

"That, my pet, I know all too well. But before I'm through with you, perhaps you'll have a glimmer of understanding of the hellish torment you've put me through. Consider this second and last mating between us a wedding present—from me to you. In the future, when you're in bed with that cold and so very... What was your mother's word? Ah, yes, it was *suitable,* wasn't it? How could I have forgotten even for a moment? When you're in bed with that eminently suitable stuffed shirt you're marrying, I want you to remember me and what you carelessly threw away eight years ago because I wasn't rich enough or suitable enough. As they say, you can't have it all in this life. You have to make choices. But very soon you'll probably realize there are some things that position and money—even a fortune as grand as the Harrisons'—can't buy, and one of them is passion like ours. So to fill in the emptiness, you'll have children—suitable ones, of course. You'll sponsor charities and be the hostess for countless social occasions to further your husband's career. You'll dress lavishly and the society columnists will write reams about your travels to Southampton or Sardinia in the summers and St. Moritz in the winter, or wherever the hell people like you go. And perhaps one day you'll discreetly take a lover on the side. But I doubt, love, that even he will be able to give you what you seek.''

Abigail listened to his passionate words and stared up at him in jumbled confusion. What was he talking about?

''You've always been able to have everything you wanted so easily that you've never wanted anything very deeply,'' he said. ''But after today, no matter how much you want me, I won't be there, little rich girl. You'll have it all—except me.''

So his lovemaking was intended as the cruelest brand of revenge.

"Grant, no. I..."

He silenced the gentle moan of pure agony that escaped her lips with a kiss that was as furiously passionate as his words.

When at last his mouth released hers, she could do nothing but numbly listen to the vibrant tones of his musical voice.

"And now, love, for the main course. I'm starving. It's been such a long time. Eight years."

"No. I don't want this."

"Liar," he whispered.

She felt his powerful tanned body poised above hers. For a long moment he stared down at her, his hot eyes burning over her naked body as though to memorize every detail of her for the lifetime he would live without her. Despite his hesitation, she knew there would be no stopping him once he decided to possess her.

Six

Occasional gusts of wind fluted beneath the eaves of the cottage. In the forest, leaves rustled and fluttered to the ground, carpeting the earth with soft layers of crunchy gold. Inside, a quiet battle was being waged beneath crinkly cotton sheets and thick angora blankets.

Grant was still, hesitating despite the surging pressure of his loins. His conscience played havoc with his desire for the woman in his arms, and a part of him regretted the brutal words that had gone before. He felt the frantic thrumming of her pulse beneath the translucent azure-tinged skin of her breasts, which jutted against his shoulders.

Her eyes were wide and luminous with intense emotion. Was it fear of him? An odd pain jabbed his heart. He felt absurdly noble toward her. She had such a gentle sensitive nature when she wasn't acting hidebound by sanctimonious Bainbridge strictures. In spite of what she'd done in the past, he realized he didn't really want to hurt her. Only a heel would trample over someone so vulnerable.

He drew a deep, ragged breath as he strove for control. With her nude beauty fused wantonly beneath his in the intimate privacy of his own bed, his pang of conscience caused him to feel as near torture as he'd ever come. Why didn't he just take her? More than anything, he longed for the explosion of male-female emotions that would blur all her Bainbridge rules in one bursting moment of torrential splendor, and she would again be just a woman in the arms of a man she loved.

That was it! What it was that he actually wanted hit him with blinding force! Sex with her wasn't going to be enough. What he really wanted was to make her love him again. That was something he couldn't force. Her love was a gift only she could bestow.

"It's your choice, Abbie," he said quietly at last. "I won't force you."

She stared up at him in sudden bewilderment.

Whatever she had expected, it was not this! Not

this new tenderness, which was even more threatening than his desire for revenge. The last shred of her resistance toward him melted.

The hands that should have pushed him away remained in a paralyzed curl against the furred warmth of his chest. Her gaze explored the curve of his sensual mouth, and she longed to feel the molten blaze of its touch. But he did not kiss her, and he wasn't going to unless she asked him to.

She was aware of the tiniest quiver of disappointment at this realization. This was what she wanted, wasn't it?—for him to relent? Yet she felt frozen, her fingers buried in the thick, curling black hair, savoring the bristly feel of it, revelling in the tight intimacy of her body with his. She caught her breath, aware of a hushed, all enveloping stillness in him, in herself, in the room. For an instant, the world seemed to stand still.

The moment of suspended time felt like an eternity; in reality it was a matter of seconds. Abigail's mind flew crazily.

She should shove him away, gather her rumpled clothes and the equally rumpled remnants of her dignity and virtue and march resolutely out to her Volkswagen. Instead she lay exactly where she was, wrapped in a sensual daze of smoldering needs with her feminine body molded indelicately to the masculine shape of his, with her traitorous body relishing the very indelicacy of its position. She was keenly aware of every place her body touched his, from her errant fingertips twining themselves in the wiry hairs of his chest instead of pushing him away, to her deliciously coiled toes pushing lightly against the vibrantly warm tops of his long, narrow feet.

He seemed to sense that her hesitation presaged acquiescence, and he brushed his fingers through her hair in slow stroking motions. The delicate eroticism of those long lean fingers kindled her awakened senses. She wanted to touch him as tenderly as he was touching her.

Was it really so wrong to give into these wonderful feelings?

Grant's hands moved over her, sliding beneath her heavy hair to caress the nape of her neck and trace the curve of her earlobe, and she could not stop the shiver of expectant pleasure that coursed through her. He knew how to touch a woman. Everywhere his fingertips touched her, her skin radiated gentle warmth.

Every part of her throbbed with fiery desire; passion washed through her with the heat of flowing lava. She felt roused to unbridled sensuality, and she was ready to abandon everything for that all-powerful emotion—love.

She knew he was going to leave her, but she wanted him so badly this one last time. Just this

once she would have what she so desperately
wanted.

He felt her body undulate provocatively beneath
his, then heard her whisper, "Kiss me."

His gaze was so intense, she closed her eyes, unable to endure the sheer force of it.

The sheets slid down their heated bodies. The
scarlet angora blanket bunched up at the foot of the
bed. Grant gathered Abigail into his arms, his male
length sprawled on top of her. He kissed her mouth,
at first slowly, with tender reverence, and then with
overwhelming urgency. Her lips parted immediately,
needing, accepting, responding, inviting.

Were their mating bodies swirling over and over
in the vast soft bed? Or was it everything else? The
room seemed to blur and spin and fade away into
sensuous nothingness, as though the two of them
were whirling far out into star-spangled space. All
was inky blackness and scarlet fire, heat and shivering cold, desire and the most splintering hunger
fired by the melting fusion of their bodies and their
searching, trembling mouths. The only reality was
Grant—the warmth of his limbs touching hers, the
powerful strength of his arms cradling her closely,
the smoldering pressure of his mouth moving leisurely over the voluptuous, pouting softness of her
lips. She returned his kisses with wanton kisses of

her own, letting her tongue mate warmly with his, all velvet intimacy and fire and wild abandonment.

She moaned softly and breathed hard, then sighed his name repeatedly against his earlobe. She uttered a confused babble of erotic love words. She whispered secretive imaginings to him. She made tantalizing confessions of womanly longings that made even the more worldly Grant flush darkly and go hot all over as though touched with flame. But he revelled in the totality of her surrender to the sensual side of her nature.

Her hands slid over his body, exploring smooth taut shoulder muscles, moving lower across his flat, hard belly, at last circling him in wonder with her fingers. He was so vibrantly hot, so magnificently virile. It had been so long, she thought, so painfully long. Eight years. And she'd been a child then and not the woman she was now. She hadn't known the glory of his love and then the grief of losing it.

Beneath her fingertips he was miraculously hard, yet satiny soft. He was so awesomely, so thrillingly a man, the only man she'd ever wanted. Her delirious joy was exquisite anguish. Her passion was a desperate pounding, a building ache growing deep within her, spreading through her, consuming her, driving her, intuitively telling her hands what to do that would most pleasure him.

He groaned, and she could hear his quick intake of breath.

Holding him, touching him, moving her hand upon his body was not enough. A furious tide of pulsating longing swept her, and she felt herself drowning in it, glorying in it, surrendering it.

Suddenly she was in an uncontrollable hurry, and all feminine shyness was obliterated.

"Quickly," she murmured, her hand guiding him to her own body. "Please, do it quickly. I...I can't wait."

"You don't have to, my love," he whispered against her open lips, possessing her mouth in the same moment that his body lowered to and possessed the fluidly soft, yielding woman in his arms.

He was as hot as a volcano, and she was on fire from the heat of him flowing into her. Every sense in her being erupted. She screamed from deep within her throat as the explosion of feeling went on and on. She was drowning, dying, living, loving.

Her excitement pulled him with her. He shed his self-control and lost himself in her. They clung to each other for a timeless moment of abandonment to supreme ecstacy.

Abigail lay still, her black lashes shuttered against the translucent smoothness of her skin. Her breathing was regular now, her heartbeats a gentle patter beneath her breasts. She felt so content, so satisfied, so utterly replete. At last, she had had what she so desperately wanted.

Idly she ran her hands through the fashionably long, auburn hair that curled against Grant's neck, enjoying the silken sensation of the loose tendrils against her fingers, the warmth of him when she caressed him.

Strange, but she didn't feel the least bit guilty.

"Well?" he said at last. She heard the smile in his voice.

"It was wonderful," she murmured, feeling strangely shy. Tears glistened at the corners of her eyes, and she blinked them back, wondering how she'd lived without him for eight long years.

"Hmm." He rolled on top of her, his hard body fitting the moist softness of hers so exactly it took her breath away. "I don't like your use of the past tense, love," he whispered huskily.

He was kissing her eyelids, dampening the long, velvet soft lashes with his tongue. At first she thought it no more than a tender gesture of affection.

Suddenly she felt the unmistakable, awesomely powerful maleness of him, and her eyes flew open in startled amazement. "Grant, didn't you?" She flushed bright red.

"Of course I did. It's not very flattering though that you have to ask," he teased.

"But I thought..." For the first time she felt guilty that she might have disappointed him. "I'm sorry I was in such a hurry."

He smoothed the hair from her damp brow. "Don't be. I loved it. I just want to do it again."

She smiled. "So do I," she said softly. "Oh, so do I."

What followed was a molten, glorious time that lasted long into the afternoon.

Seven

Abigail woke up slowly, rising languidly from the deep warmth of sleep like a dormant, winged creature awakening within its chrysalis, pushing through a series of varying states of semiconsciousness. Her first perception was of utter silence both in the house and outside. The cottage was wrapped in dark gray stillness.

Everything was the same, yet everything was different because she was different. She was a woman sated with love and love's fulfillment. The emptiness of eight years was no more. She smiled and blushed as wanton memories caught her in their swirl. She remembered strong arms shaping her body to fit masculine contours; she recalled emotions flaming out of control, words spoken, promises given. Were they real? Had she? Had he? She searched for him then, wanting to mold her body to his and luxuriate against the splendid warmth of him. But even as she stirred, the vague sensation that something was wrong overcame her.

She was alone. It was something she felt even before she opened her eyes and saw the rumpled hollow of his pillow where his dark head had lain so near her own. While she had slept, he had gone out—without her. At this realization she felt a vague, painful twist in her throat. When she reached over and touched the soft cotton pillowcase, the fabric was cool beneath her fingertips. The pleasing scent of his skin lingering on the material made her all the more poignantly aware of his absence.

He must have been gone for some time. She felt a ridiculous sense of crushing abandonment. Why had he left her? Where had he gone? And when? Slowly she rose, the sheets falling away from her nude form, her toes touching the cool stone floor. Her head ached with questions.

She stared about the room, and everything reminded her of Grant, from its orderliness and simplicity to the masculine taste of the furnishings. The windowpanes were shiny clean, the walls freshly painted a pale beige, the brown curtains blending with the darker color of the bed coverings. On a well-polished captain's chair beneath the window sat her neatly opened suitcase, its contents in the same scramble she'd left them in. Grant must have brought her bag in from her car before he'd left.

How could she have slept through the popping of her brass bindings and the creaking of leather when he'd opened it? Well, she had. He must have deliberately taken pains to do everything noiselessly so as not to awaken her.

Feeling increasingly disconsolate, she tiptoed gracefully into the bath and drew a tub of warm water. She flushed, remembering the wanton splendor of the bath Grant had given her during one of their sessions of lovemaking. As she slid into the tub, she could almost feel his lean fingers exploring every feminine part of her. She trembled at the delicious memory.

She bathed leisurely, hoping to hear his car in the drive, his footsteps falling heavily on the living room floor, his deep voice calling out her name. But he did not come, and she lay in the tub with her mind a disturbed drift of sensual images that were punctuated by feelings of profound loss. She pondered all that had happened between them. At last the bath water became so chilled that she either had to freshen it with more hot water or get out.

She dressed in a pair of turquoise corduroy slacks

and a cotton checked blouse and white pullover. Not exactly clothes Rosalind would have approved of, but they were neat and functional. She'd planned to see Aunt Peggy, not her mother; if Aunt Peggy had a choice between a designer original and a garage-sale bargain, she'd steer clear of the designer piece every time.

An hour passed in which Abigail tidied the bed and prepared herself a bowl of canned soup. Still, Grant did not return. She stared at her empty soup bowl and listened to the silence. The fact that he hadn't come back was beginning to seem increasingly ominous to her. Did he want nothing more to do with her? Was that why he'd left? She choked back a sob. His leaving didn't have to mean anything, she tried to reassure herself, but then her doubts tormented her once again. Where was he?

Their lovemaking had been wonderful, but everything that had happened between them had happened so fast, it could be that he thought it a mistake.

For the first time Abigail thought guiltily of Harold and her mother. She remembered the note she'd written her mother; she recalled Harold's implicit faith in her. Harold did not deserve such shabby treatment. She was engaged to marry him, and look what she had done! Even as she indulged her conscience, some part of her was more honest. Her feelings for Grant were so miraculously special that she simply couldn't deny them. It was Harold, not Grant, who was the wrong man.

Agonizing seconds slowly passed, and though she tried to keep herself busy by doing inconsequential chores around the house, her emotions were building explosively inside her. She heard every sound in the forest and every one of the few automobiles that whizzed past on the country road.

Two hours later she was so angry she was no longer dwelling on Grant as a special miracle but as a suitable nominee for "heel of the year."

He had left her again, without so much as a word, just as he had left her eight years ago. Oh, she was such a fool where he was concerned! She'd thrown herself unwisely into his bed. But despite her utter stupidity, why couldn't he have had the decency at least to say goodbye? Even as she imagined the goodbye she realized that vision was equally galling, perhaps more so than his leaving. Far better that he had simply left, as if she were no more than a cheap conquest to him. She choked back the lump in her throat. There was a terrible taste in her mouth, as though she'd swallowed a very bitter pill that hadn't quite gone down.

Suddenly she was glad that Grant hadn't stayed. What could they have said to each other, anyway? Would he have smiled that showy white smile of his as he mouthed some inanity that was more cruel than a stake driven through her softest tissue? She could almost hear the savage irony of his deep, melodious drawl wringing her heart as dry of its life force as if it were a rag he had wrung and slapped indifferently against a washtub. "Hey, you were great, babe, almost like old times." Or something simpler and more casual. "See you around. Maybe…" "Thanks for dropping by" or "Let's do this again sometime." At that last she cringed.

The walls of the kitchen blurred as she shoved her chair back from the table. She brushed her glistening tears aside, not wanting it to be heartbreak she felt, but anger.

Damn him! She wasn't going to grieve! Not for him, not ever again! Blindly she raced toward the bedroom, nursing the blaze of fury until it swelled into a roaring, all-consuming conflagration of emotions that burned away her sorrow.

Well, she wouldn't be here waiting if he chose to come back!

She tried not to look at the bed as she packed, for when she did she envisioned Grant's dark, compelling virility all too easily. Her fingers began to tremble. She tried not to remember the intimacies and the soaring passion she'd shared with him in this unpretentious bedroom. But it was impossible to put all that totally from her mind. Her body still ached feverishly from all the lovemaking; it had been too glorious. The afterglow had scarcely dimmed, and that made her all the more frustrated with herself.

She slammed her suitcase shut and stomped out of the house with a great show of determination. She would go back to Pittsburgh, where she belonged—back to the bleakly rigid order of the Bainbridges, where pain and sorrow and loss could be carefully locked away.

As the Volkswagen sputtered to life and rolled jerkily down the drive, she told herself how lucky she was to be returning to her safe world, where civilized people behaved by rules.

It was night when Grant's ancient blue Valiant drove up the leaf-strewn, rutted driveway, heedless of the bumps and sloshing mud holes and their effect on his worn shocks. The only thing he saw was that Abigail's canary yellow Volkswagen was no longer parked by the cottage.

So, she was gone… His chest constricted in unwanted pain. Never had his house looked so lost and forlorn beneath the brooding darkness of the trees. Never had he felt less like returning to it and going inside—alone.

He frowned as he kicked the front door open with his boot and strode wearily inside. He shrugged out of his sheepskin jacket, not bothering to call her name. The last thing he wanted to hear was his unanswered voice reverberating like a hollow sound inside a drum, reminding him of his acute need for a woman who could never really want him for the person he was.

Why had he left then, if he hadn't wanted to find her gone when he came back? He'd known when he'd walked out the door that that was a risk he was taking. But he'd needed to get away, to think about what had happened. Besides, it had been his way of making it easy on himself. If it was her intention to leave, it would have been even more painful if he'd had to watch her walk out of his house.

The logical side of his nature wanted her to be gone and accepted her departure as inevitable. But despite the rightness of her leaving, her absence tore at him with the pain of an amputated limb.

He remembered her exquisite face, her over-large blue eyes shining up at him when he'd held her in his arms with her body pressed beneath his. He could still see her mouth, soft and sweet as the petal of a rose. He imagined her smile, and he could almost feel his mouth claiming those hot, upturned lips, which parted so invitingly to accept the intimate invasion of his tongue.

"Damn!" Why had he fallen in love with that Bainbridge siren, who was wild as a tornado in his bed and cool and brittlely proper out of it as an aristocrat's china tea set—and just as useless? Why had he stupidly confessed to Peggy that he wanted to see Abigail again, thereby bringing all of this upon himself with new freshness?

He had told himself he wanted to see Abigail again to teach her a lesson, he reminded himself. He'd wanted her to know what she was giving up when she walked down the aisle with her suitable Harrison and became his suitable wife. And chagrined, he admitted to himself he'd needed to prove to himself how little he felt for her. Some lesson! He imagined her serenely driving away in her yellow car. Instead of his teaching her a lesson, he was the one to learn again how difficult life would be without her. She had escaped untouched, back to the safety of her secure life.

"Damn her!" He strode into the kitchen and pulled a beer out of the refrigerator.

He had gone out to get a perspective on his feelings and had returned to have a long, serious talk with Abigail on the chance they might be able to work something out. But he hadn't really held much hope that they could. Now that she was gone, he accepted that all was lost. He would never again chase after her.

He opened the refrigerator door again and pulled out the entire six-pack of beer. To hell with sobriety! To hell with the world! To hell with Abigail Bainbridge!

Carrying the unopened beers in his hands, he walked to his bedroom and switched on the television to a station that carried old movies. Broodingly he observed the credits for *The Graduate* without a flicker of interest; his attention was still focused on Abigail. He sipped from one of the cans, plunking the others down on the table beside the bed.

Tomorrow he would start working again. He knew he would be very busy—hopefully too busy to think, since the doctor who'd retired from the clinic had told him there was too much work for one man to do. For the first time in the last month, Grant welcomed the thought of work; after Africa and his work there in the jungle hospital, he'd almost dreaded plunging into his career again. He had worked tirelessly, ceaselessly for three years under the most primitive conditions until in the end he'd been so totally exhausted he hadn't been able to face setting up a practice on a permanent basis without first taking several weeks of rest. Now, as far as he was concerned, tomorrow couldn't come quickly enough.

The Bainbridge living room reflected Rosalind's favorite period—eighteenth-century European, mostly French, and visitors instantly had the feeling that every item, from the hand-woven carpets to the porcelains and collection of writing desks, had been

selected not only for its beauty, but for its invest-
ment value. The room was so formal and its contents
so valuable that such boisterous miscreants as children and big dogs had never been allowed to cross
its threshold. It was scarcely a place for relaxation,
though Rosalind was proud of it. It had been the
scene of many a Bainbridge lecture to a certain tow-
headed young Bainbridge who'd squirmed uneasily
amidst such formal grandeur.

Harold sat stiffly upon one of the Louis XV chairs
beneath a dark oil painting by the late American
artist Howard Logan Hildenbrandt. With an expression of pompous gravity dutifully pasted upon his
freckled features, he was sipping coffee from a rare
demitasse cup pretending to listen to Rosalind as she
spoke of plans for his forthcoming wedding in two
days. In reality the sharp voice was a dull drone in
the back of his mind, and it was Abigail he observed
with intense fascination and concern. She sat across
from him in the uncomfortable twin of his own
Louis XV chair. On her slender fingers, folded
primly in her lap, glittered the magnificent Harrison
diamond. The sight of it on her delicate hand, a hand
he noted was trembling, caused Harold to puff up
with pride and a curious proprietary feeling. In two
days this beautiful woman would be his wife, and
she was so exactly right for this honor that he could
scarcely believe his good fortune. He admired her

cool, poised beauty, her elegance, her quietness. She exuded good breeding and restraint.

Despite his great wealth, Harold had always been shy toward women, never knowing what to say to them. All too often in his past relationships with them, they had taken the aggressive role, and he had felt virtually emasculated. For years Lauren Carlyle had led him around as disdainfully as though she had a ring through his nose. But a year ago he'd met Abigail at the Symphony Ball. She'd been so quiet and shy that he'd felt all-man, and he'd summoned the courage to break off with Lauren and court Abigail instead. He'd wanted to protect Abigail and take care of her. On that first night, he'd known he wanted to marry her, but he'd sensed a reticence in her manner that made him go slowly with her. He understood reticence; until his relationship with Abigail, he'd felt it toward most of the women he'd dated.

With Abigail, he was the boss, and this had become a heady sensation. His new power had gone immediately to his head, and although he didn't know it, he was rapidly becoming a tyrant. He only knew that when he gave his perfectly reasonable orders, she sweetly complied. At least she had until the last few days.

Ever since Abigail had returned a week ago from that spur-of-the-moment trip that she'd never adequately explained, she had been different—worrisomely so. There were new barriers between them that hadn't been there since the beginning of their relationship. Rosalind had tried to brush those missing days aside as though they made no difference, but it was Rosalind's obvious fear that most unnerved him.

Where had Abigail gone? And what had happened to her?

Abigail had always been quiet, but now she said nothing unless she was asked a direct question. When he gave his orders, she dutifully listened as she always had, but now she almost always forgot to obey them. Tonight at Poli's she'd scarcely touched her lobster, and later at Heinz Hall she'd watched *I Pagliacci* without a glimmer of her usual enthusiasm.

Other things worried him. Frequently Abigail lost the drift of their conversations, and he noticed that when he touched her now or tried to kiss her, she trembled and pulled away as though deeply agitated. He was beside himself with concern. Something was wrong, and the last thing he needed to complicate his already complex life was a troublesome wife. He'd wanted her because he'd considered her a pleasant, easily dominated companion as well as a magnificent social asset. After all, she was a Bainbridge. But this withdrawn, tense creature disturbed him.

Despite her obvious unhappiness, Abigail was more remarkably beautiful than ever. Her translucent skin was flushed with a strange restlessness, and her vivid eyes were even more arrestingly brilliant. In a room filled with fragile, lavish ornaments, she was the most exquisitely precious of them all. Tonight she was dressed simply, wearing a stunning design by Adrienne Vittadini of which Harold highly approved. Every aspect of her appearance spelled class, and he was proud of the way heads turned when she was on his arm. A clinging, celery green mohair sweater embroidered with seashells of chenille clung to her ample breasts, and tight-fitting glossy kid leather pants of a matching shade molded her slender legs.

"And so, children, I suppose that concludes everything," Rosalind finished as briskly as a schoolteacher. "Questions?"

Abigail stared at her hands in her lap. Harold stared at Abigail, first at her hands and then at her breasts. Rosalind stared at them both with an air of hopeless resignation, as though wondering if they'd heard a word she'd said.

Later when Harold and Abigail were alone, Harold said, "You've hardly said a word, Abigail. Is anything wrong?"

"I suppose I'm just overwhelmed by it all," Abigail lied, forcing herself to meet his steady gaze. "But I'll be all right the day of the wedding. I promise." *Would she? Would she ever be all right again?*

"I'm not worried about the wedding, you goose!" he said irritably, wishing he could force some animation into her. "I'm worried about you."

Abigail made no response, and they lapsed into frozen silence. Half an hour later when she ushered him to the door, the painful awkwardness was still there between them.

The minute he had gone, Abigail retreated hastily up the stairs to her bedroom; her mother had forced her to agree to residing in her old room until the wedding. Rosalind had said it was more convenient, but in reality they both knew that it was to prevent another alarming disappearance.

Abigail shut the door quietly and faced the numbing emptiness of her heart with weakening resolve. Her plan to marry Harold in spite of everything wasn't working. She could barely speak to him, barely tolerate his touch…after Grant's. Besides that, she felt terribly guilty every time she was with Harold—their relationship was a sham. He thought she loved him. She'd thought so, too, but now she knew she was only deeply fond of him, as she would have been of a much beloved brother. Oh, what was she going to do? Tonight when her mother had gone on and on about the wedding plans she'd almost blurted there would be no wedding. But how did one call off a grand society wedding that Rosalind Bainbridge had spent months organizing? How could she hurt and embarrass Harold when she remembered how terribly patient he'd been toward her? Abigail thought of Michael; she thought of what Rosalind might do if she spoiled everything by a last-hour confession about her feelings for Grant. There were those dreadful boarding schools Rosalind could send Michael to.

Abigail threw herself across her bed, indifferent to the elaborate bedspread, mindless of the fact that in this house it was a rule that no one ever sat on bedspreads; doing so made them wear more quickly, and they were so terribly, terribly expensive that even the Bainbridges could ill afford to replace them too frequently. When one got into bed, bedspreads were to be carefully folded and tidily placed aside.

What was she going to do? But why did she even ask that question? She couldn't go back to Grant. Had he called even once? Aunt Peggy had said over the phone that when she had seen Grant he had not even mentioned her. It was all too obvious that he didn't want to make any sort of commitment to her. Harold was ready to marry her, and in time, surely things would be the same as they had been before between Harold and herself. They would, as her mother said so frequently, "build a life together." She couldn't spend her life pining after a lost dream, especially not when she had her child and the thrill of being his mother was at last a reality within her grasp.

Grant strode wearily into the kitchen and sat his sack of groceries on the table. He ripped the stethoscope from his neck and hooked it on the back of a chair. Then he pulled a beer from the sack as well as a gourmet TV dinner, which he placed in the microwave. He'd worked tirelessly in the village clinic every day since Abigail had left. Tonight was his first night off, and he was too exhausted to cook, much less go out and eat, just as he'd been too tired to plan a date with a certain bright young woman who he knew would have gone out with him. He faced the first evening alone since Abbie had left. Well, he had to do that sometime, he thought, lifting his beer in a mock salute.

"To you, Abbie." His dark gaze fell to the newspaper, which lay open to the society pages that contained pictures of her and Harold. "I'm sure you'll make a very illustrious couple."

He had read the articles outlining the elaborate wedding plans that were scheduled for tomorrow.

Tomorrow. Already? Was tomorrow really her wedding day? He'd worked so hard that the days had passed in a savage blur of pregnant women and children with colds and stomach aches.

In a painful stupor of anguish and self-loathing he ate dinner, downing far more beers than usual as he did so. He rarely drank much, both because of his profession and because there were other things he preferred to do. But tonight he could, because he wasn't on call, and he wanted to blot out all thought.

He went into his bedroom and flipped on the TV. "Damn! Not *The Graduate* again!" he muttered furiously, but he wouldn't have been happy with any selection. He switched channels and then, discovering nothing remotely endurable, turned the set off with a violent twist of the knob and decided to go for a long walk in the forest.

An hour later he returned. The walk had been a mistake; he'd done nothing but think of Abbie. It was driving him mad! The silence in the house closed in around him, and suddenly he wished he was back at the hospital so he wouldn't have to think anymore. He flipped the television back on to *The Graduate* and forced himself to concentrate on the dialogue and Benjamen's panic.

It was such a ridiculous story, Grant thought with unusual cynicism, since he usually liked ridiculous stories even when he'd seen them many times. Making it first with the mother and then the daughter, and then determining to marry the daughter in spite of the mother, Benjamen seemed to Grant an even worse fool than himself. With a feeling of smug superiority, he watched Benjamen frantically try to win the daughter away from her fiancé. Grant even laughed as the poor idiot grabbed the bride in the church after her wedding vows. And he roared with derisive laughter when Benjamen jammed a large cross through the doors of the church and ran off with his girl. No one but an utter fool could be that desperate about a woman.

No one but an utter fool.

Eight

Beams of pastel light slanted through the magnificent stained glass windows, painting glorious, brilliant patterns on soaring beams and flying arches. Beneath this splendor, a quaking groom with raspberry freckles and his eight attendants stood at the altar in their black tuxes, looking like a row of giant, terrified penguins. The air was richly perfumed with the intoxicating scent of the flowers festooning the sanctuary—orchids, roses, gladiolas, carnations, irises.

The wedding march was playing, and twin four-year-old ring bearers, suddenly shy from self-importance, ambled in ramshackle fashion down the

aisle, their gait as lazily aimless as that of two
stuffed geese on a stroll. But their foot-dragging,
scarlet-faced passage brought smiles and whispers—
"The little darlings." "Oh, look, aren't they precious!"

Behind this pair of showstoppers floated an or-
ganza army of smiling bridesmaids, blushing prettily
in their regal finery, in turn followed by two bouncing flower girls, who looked like fluffy pink sugar
confections as they tossed primroses down upon the
red plush carpeting for the bride to walk upon.

The bridal attendants shuffled to find their posi-
tions at the front of the church. The beat of the music was stepped up. An expectant hush fell on the
distinguished crowd smugly nestled amidst the extravagant rumples of silver foxes, minks and soft,
inky sables as they swiveled on their red velvet-
cushioned pews, straining to look back up the aisle
in anticipation of the bride.

All was in readiness for the grandest of entrances!
This was the moment Rosalind Bainbridge had spent
a lifetime waiting for. Twining her fingers through
her grandson, Michael's hair, she stole a proud
glance toward the back of the church.

The wedding march seemed to go on and on,
louder and with growing insistence, but no angel in
white appeared in the empty doorway. Necks were
beginning to hurt, and a queer murmur stole through

the crowd. Rosalind's entire body began to ache. Every silvered hair follicle seemed to pull at her scalp, but her iron smile never faltered in its brightness, and her gray eyes remained glued with admirable determination on the open doors at the back of the sanctuary. She clutched Michael's tiny hand as if it were a lifeline.

In the church foyer, Abigail stood frozen with pain. The music throbbed through her. She tried to take a step, but her legs wouldn't function. Her merry widow was so tight it pinched when she tried to take a deep breath. Something hard and dry was clogging her throat, and she couldn't swallow. For an instant she was so terrified, she felt as if she were dying.

How could she go in there and marry Harold—in front of all those people? The magnitude of her painful dilemma was sweeping her, and she couldn't go forward or backward. She must be going mad! At last she was aware of her body moving as though it had assumed a will of its own. The utterly black moment seemed to have passed; she squared her slender shoulders with determination. She was a Bainbridge after all, and Bainbridges did what was expected of them even when their hearts were bursting with pain.

Scarcely knowing what she did, Abigail glided fearfully down the aisle with her train trailing behind

her like the white froth of a wave rippling against
the blood red streamer. But her face was a still and
gray as a corpse's, her lipstick too vivid in contrast,
like bright, new paint on a doll's face. When Abigail
reached Harold, she managed to stop and stood
shaking beside him, but she couldn't lift her eyes to
meet his. A strange tension gripped her. Between
his abundant raspberry freckles, Harold whitened
with nerves himself. Something seemed dreadfully,
dreadfully wrong.

Mercifully, Rosalind's second cousin began to
sing from the pulpit, covering the awkward moment
so adroitly that soon is was forgotten. Rosalind listened to the sweet, clear notes filling the church and
beamed with benign pleasure, the pain in her hair
follicles lessening.

The ladies present, who were connoisseurs of
grand weddings, noted every detail and were
amazed. Everything was utterly perfect—the bride
so spectacularly a beauty in a gown of exquisite and
costly design, the bridegroom tall and so terribly
rich, the lovely bridal attendants so harmoniously
gowned, the church so lavishly decorated it would
have been indecent were the arrangements not done
in such impeccable taste. And the reception afterward was to be held on the Bainbridge estate in an
elaborate pavilion that had been especially erected
for the occasion and was rumored to be a veritable

palace. The grand ladies nodded approvingly, envying Rosalind Bainbridge her flair for the ornate yet brilliantly tasteful. It would not be easy to beat an occasion such as this.

Just as Rosalind sat basking in the glory of her achievement, this blissful state of social perfection was smashed as totally as a priceless vase dashed deliberately to bits on concrete pavement by a sadistic vandal. The floating soprano notes of the sentimental song were rent by the most anguished cry any member of that elegant crowd had ever heard.

"Abbie! Abbie! Don't do it!"

"My God!" This was a terse whisper muttered by Rosalind as she twisted and saw the virile, unshaven ghost from her worst nightmare materialise before her disbelieving eyes in the middle of the aisle at the back of the church. He stood tall and broad shouldered, pridefully arrogant despite his deplorable dishabille. "It can't be!" Rosalind stared at him as though he were a monster striding slowly down the aisle toward her daughter. "But it is!"

Everyone watched popeyed and spellbound, silenced by this moment of high drama.

Abigail whirled. Out of the thousand illustrious personages assembled in the church, she saw only one human being—Grant!

Instantly her face was lit with that rare radiance of true love. She noticed ridiculous things—the fact that he was the only man present without formal attire. He was overpoweringly virile in faded jeans and a scarlet velour pullover that emphasized every ripple of hard muscle on his long, lean frame. Why hadn't he at least shaved? And was he deliberately wearing those mud-spattered cowboy boots just to shock everyone?

But she didn't care. All that mattered was that he had come.

"Grant." Her awed whisper could have been heard by a spider clinging in the rafters, so hushed was the church.

She bunched her long dress up in her trembling fingers and flew down the aisle into his arms. She was aware of his strong arms circling her waist as he lifted her up in the air and swirled her above his dark head in a moment replete with loving triumph.

She was flying, soaring, glorying as he slowly lowered her and kissed her upon the lips with a hard kiss that was the most intensely private of her life, despite the crowd of one thousand gaping guests.

There was an audible gasp, and the lovers remembered they were not alone. Their lips parted reluctantly, and he set her from him. But his black eyes lingered on her face. His hand reached up to caress the reddened spot on her chin where the stubble of his beard had scratched her.

Harold, suddenly come to life, was racing down

the aisle toward them, whether to seize his bride or to demand an explanation of this outrageous behavior, no one knew. Rosalind's silvery bulk was right behind him, plowing full steam ahead with the determination of a battleship draped in gray satin bearing down upon its target.

A ripple of expectant excitement stirred through the crowd.

Grant seized Abigail's hand tightly in his. "Run, Abbie, we've got to run." And together they sped out of the sanctuary, stumbling out into the crisp October air clambering down the fifty marble steps, trampling across the manicured lawn to the narrow side street where Grant had parked his car. Right behind them galloped Rosalind, Harold, his best man, and many others in hot, furious pursuit.

Grant stuffed Abigail and her dress into his car and loped to the driver's side. His face purple with humiliation and fury, Harold was pounding against the glass window as Grant slid into the car, started the engine, and shoved the gear into forward. The Valiant lurched toward freedom. Abigail whirled and watched Harold and the others, who were swarming like a horde of angry bees, grow smaller and smaller as the car sped away. Then as Grant squealed around a sharp corner, she was thrown across the car seat toward him, and she felt his arms slide possessively around her slim shoulders. She sank breathlessly against his hard muscular arm.

"That was as good as an old cowboy movie," Grant murmured softly. "I felt like we were being chased by a tribe of wild Indians!"

"A tribe of wild Bainbridges is an equally rare sight."

"I didn't know your mother could run like that!"

"Let's not talk about mother!" Abigail knew thinking of her mother and the pain she must be going through would spoil everything with guilt.

"Good idea."

"Can we go by my apartment, so I can get out of this dress?"

He smiled. "Just like a woman to be thinking of clothes at a time like this!"

"Grant!"

"You'll have to give me directions, and we shouldn't stay but a minute. No telling who might show up."

When they entered Abigail's studio, Grant stared with amazement at the clutter of canvases and paint pots, the teetering stacks of art books on dusty tables and the daubs of paint spattered on the floor.

"This place is a mess."

"So I've been told," Abigail agreed unworriedly. She was clutching her train and the flounces of her dress as tightly to her as she could, so the precious satin wouldn't touch anything dirty. "Quit feeling superior and help me out of this dress!"

"My pleasure." His voice went soft and silky. His black eyes glinted with disturbing intensity.

A delicious shiver sped through her. "That's not what I meant!" she snapped, trying to show off the spell of his male magnetism.

"Then, maybe I can do something to change your mind," he turned lazily, grinning down at her, reading her all too easily.

"And what might that be?"

"I can think of lots of possibilities, can't you, and all of them are so enticingly erotic, aren't they, my sweet?"

Abigail couldn't wholly dismiss the sensual visions his words evoked, but she tried valiantly. He kept looking at her in that special way that made her heart flutter; his direct, unwavering gaze brought a strange heat to her skin. She tossed her head and looked away from him, not wanting to confront the strange, urgent emotion she read in his eyes.

Still holding her gown bunched to herself so that it wouldn't brush against anything, Abigail picked her way daintily across the littered studio with the careful movements of a fastidious cat tiptoeing across a wet floor. Despite her most fervent wish not to think of Rosalind, she couldn't help herself. She knew that if her mother could see her now in her designer gown amidst this paint and clutter, she would surely collapse from a heart spell.

"Let's go into my bedroom, so I won't get paint on this dress," she said quickly.

"This is getting better by the minute," came Grant's warm, suggestive drawl from behind her.

Just his voice could make her feel as if her stomach were dissolving.

He, on the other hand, was watching the graceful swaying motion of her hips, the ripple of clinging satin outlining every entrancing movement of her feminine shape.

He stepped into her bedroom, and Abigail was immediately conscious of him dwarfing everything else in it. He was right behind her, standing so close to her she could feel the heat of him. Feeling strangely disquieted, she turned and looked up into his eyes, and though neither spoke, they were both aware of a new, electric intimacy between them.

The full impact of what they had done was upon them.

Abigail looked at him and remembered what she'd done to Harold, to her mother. But Grant looked so dear to her. Even in his unshaven state he was devastatingly handsome, so casually male. He had the look of a satyr, with his black, knowledge-able eyes and his rumpled dark hair, which fell sex-ily across his tanned brown and black eyebrows.

Who could blame her for being insane about such a bronzed hunk?

He was so compellingly attractive that suddenly she couldn't speak. She could only stare up at him with curious bewilderment, her heart skipping faster. His dark eyes ravaged her and the leisurely bold movement of his gaze sliding over her figure, lingering on her ample breasts, set her skin wantonly afire beneath the smooth, cool satin.

His tanned hand reached out and gently brushed the side of her face, his fingers tracing the delicate line of her jaw and then disappearing into the warm radiant gold of her hair.

"In the church," he murmured wonderingly, "when I called your name, I was afraid you might not come with me. I thought I might make that ridiculous scene, ruin your wedding, all to no purpose but to play the fool. But you did come with me. Why, Abbie?"

His fingertips knew exactly how to touch a woman, and she was keenly aware of them as they played with her hair.

"I...I'm not sure," she said at last. "I just felt... that I had to."

He laughed softly, his triumph and delight mingling in the velvet resonance of that warm male sound. She felt mesmerized as his finger affectionately touched the tip of her nose and then moved downward to explore the soft curving allure of her wet mouth. Her scalp was still atingle from his touch.

"I still can't believe you came with me," he admitted. "Does it give you any satisfaction to know how uncertain I was and still am of you, Abbie?"

"No," she whispered truthfully. "But I'm just as uncertain of you. I...I don't know if I'll ever be able to trust you."

"Nor I you."

"And yet today we behaved like two crazy kids very much in love. Where do we go from here?" she asked.

"We'll have to take it a day at a time, I guess," he replied, removing his hand from the corner of her lips. "I only hope you don't decide you made a mistake."

"That's a risk we both took, didn't we?" she asked, moving away from him and pretending to lift the hair from the back of her neck. But in reality she was rubbing her skin, trying to erase the tingling from her neck and scalp where he had been touching her. She wiped her hand against her lips as though to wipe away his touch there as well.

He watched the way the movement of her hand made the satin pulled across the curve of her breasts shimmer.

"If we're going to get you out of that dress, we'd

better get at it,'' he said changing the subject abruptly. "Besides, if we stay here much longer, we may have unwelcome visitors. Turn around and let me undo the zipper," he ordered.

"I'm afraid you're in for a bit of a surprise," she said archly, tilting her smiling face toward his, observing the sensual curve of his mouth as she did so.

"I hope it's pleasant," he mused, and she felt his hot gaze linger upon her lips just as she'd been looking at his. Inadvertently she moistened them with a quick swirl of her tongue.

He drew a quick, deep breath as he watched the movement of her pink tongue.

"There's no zipper," she tossed tartly, bringing his attention back to the matter at hand. "Buttons."

Grant stared in sudden horror at the row of tiny satin balls that ran like a line of beading down the length of her spine. "Hell, Abbie, there must be a million of them!" he grumbled, applying his hands to the intricacies of the top button.

His fingers were warm against the naked skin of her nape, his touch sending a shock of pleasing sensations radiating through her body.

"Only a hundred," she said sweetly, trying unsuccessfully to ignore the way his hands lazily scorched her heated skin.

"Only?"

"Patience," she whispered with a feline purr.

"Who are you to tout that virtue?" he murmured huskily against her velvet earlobe, reminding her of her lack of it in sexual matters. Grant painstakingly slipped a loop off one offending satin-covered ball after another, exposing more warm, delectable skin. Suddenly on impulse he lifted her hair, lowered his lips and kissed her gently upon the bare flesh at the base of her neck.

She felt his lips nibbling in slow, erotic circles that were so pleasurable she didn't mind his bristly beard scratching her. It only made him seem all the more male.

"Grant, you'll never finish at this rate," she forced herself to say.

"You taste so delicious, I may have to eat a little of you after every button. My just reward!"

"You're going to get your just reward if you don't hurry and Rosalind and Harold decide to come here!"

"I'm quaking in my mud-stained boots," he murmured dryly. "But you're right." He began unbuttoning her gown at a quicker pace. "I'm only so obedient because I'm in no mood to share you."

"Grant," she said suddenly, feeling a strange, bewildering desire sweep her like flames of fire racing in a headlong path. "Kiss me!"

"I thought you'd never ask."

He drew her hard against him, crushing layers of satin and lace. She felt the smoldering heat of him even though the thickness of the fabric. She felt him shaking, and her own body began to tremble as his excitement communicated itself to her.

His warm, strong hands slid over her body, and he pressed her so closely against himself that she felt the hard muscles of his thighs against her own, much softer hips. Even before his mouth touched hers, she was limp and dizzy with desire.

Abigail's arms curled around his neck in complete abandon, her senses reigning supreme. He moved his mouth across her face, kissing every part of her—her eyes, her nose, the side of her cheek, the sensitive skin beneath her earlobe. Then his mouth swooped down once more to capture her upturned lips, his searching mouth stirring every fiber in her being. The familiar taste of his warm mouth was wildly intoxicating.

Her hands moved over his body, savoring the feel of his rippling muscles. He was so incredibly hot, so virile, all male.

Grant pulled her down onto the bed. His searing mouth followed the delicate curve of her chin to the hollow her throat. The beat of her heart throbbed against his lips. She felt his hands lifing the voluminous, satin skirts, roaming over her legs, between her thighs, pushing her petticoats aside, sliding her panty hose down her slender legs.

His hands spanned her waist, lifting and arching her body to fit his own awesome masculine contours. But her dress twisted and crunched, getting in the way; it seemed to be everywhere—lace scratching sensitive skin, satin tangling between legs.

"This damn dress," he muttered. "There's so much of it. I can't touch you where I want to...the way I want to."

She was scarcely listening, and his lips took hers in another breathless, exploring kiss. His body forced her backward upon the bed; his weight pinned her beneath him, as he followed her down. She was molded to the hard male length of him, their bodies pressed together in wanton abandonment. Abigail had never wanted him more intensely than she did at this moment. She was surrendering every part of herself—her body as well as her heart and soul.

"Oh, Grant," she moaned feverishly. "I can't wait..."

"You never can," he murmured with a sexy chuckle against her hot wet mouth. "But all these buttons...I'm afraid you'll have to either settle for kissing or wait while I unhook them."

"Forget the buttons," she muttered fiercely.

"I've never made love to a runaway bride in her wedding gown," he whispered.

The image his words provoked was powerfully erotic.

"As they say, my darling," she purred, "there's a first time for everything."

The urgency he heard in her voice excited him so thoroughly that he forgot the dress and concentrated on the woman. Nothing compelled him so much as Abigail when she lost herself, when she forgot she was a Bainbridge, when she threw off the strictures of that careful Bainbridge rearing and gloried in the wondrous pleasure of her sexuality.

Grant's hard mouth ravaged Abigail's with savage completeness, and she felt herself spiraling in a blaze of total surrender.

Nine

"**I** can't believe you're really a doctor!" Abigail said, her boots crunching into the thick damp leaves as she walked beside Grant on Aunt Peggy's game preserve.

They walked beneath giant aromatic pines, hemlock, oak and maple trees. They came to a place where gray tree limbs scratched the sky, their stark, naked branches appearing twisted and eerie without their cloak of golden leaves. It was amazing that all the leaves could have fallen in the short time that Abigail had been away.

"It's obvious you're deeply impressed, but I'm not sure whether I can take it as a compliment," he said dryly, amusement lacing his deep tone. "It sounds like you don't have much faith in my ability to be one." He deliberately shortened his long strides so she could keep up with him more easily.

"Oh, it isn't that, Grant," she said quickly. "Aunt Peggy just didn't mention that Dr. Adams had retired and you were taking his place in the clinic. You didn't say anything about it yourself when I was here before."

"We were busy though, weren't we?"

His sudden white smile was suggestive, and she remembered their long wanton day in bed together.

"I'm afraid I'm not the kind of doctor the Bainbridges would approve of," he said mildly as he walked beside her. "I'm not going to specialize and affiliate myself with a big name hospital. I'm just a simple, old-fashioned family practitioner. I didn't go into medicine to make money, but because I wanted to help people. I know that sounds naive, but I never had much in the way of things in my life. And I've found that I haven't missed them. I thought I could do the most good in a small town where there weren't any other doctors. With Dr. Adams gone, people out here were going without some of the basic medical care they needed. What I mean is, that unless a person's really sick, he thinks before he drives fifty miles into a city to see a doctor. So a lot of routine tests that could have detected serious illness in their early stages go undone. I've always liked this part of Pennsylvania, and I was ready to start a practice. You see, after spending the past three years in Africa practicing medicine in very primitive conditions deep in a jungle in Nigeria, I was ready to come home and settle down.''

She was listening, completely absorbed in what he was saying. He stopped walking, and so did she. She felt his fingers circle hers, and he brought her palm to his mouth. Turning it over, he kissed it. A tremor of sensation went through her. He was staring at her intently, her curled fingers still pressed against his warm lips.

''I still can't believe you're here…right now… with me,'' he said very quietly.

''Neither can I,'' she answered just as quietly.

''It won't be easy, Abbie.''

''I know, but I feel we have to try,'' she admitted. ''I can't go on with my life, wondering if I could have been happy with you.''

''We've hurt each other in the past,'' he said vaguely, seeing no point in throwing up the specifics of her terrible betrayal. He was willing to give her the benefit of the doubt. She had been young then.

''Yes.'' She, too, felt too generous to bring up the past and his treachery…and her eight lost years…and Michael. She couldn't bring Michael into this yet. Not when her relationship with Grant was still so uncertain.

"I'm never going to offer you the life of glamour Harold could."

A gust of wind swept through the forest, stirring the forest floor into a flurry of gold. She shivered. As a rush of leaves fluttered past them, he drew her deeply into his arms to warm her.

"I'm not sure I ever wanted a life of glamour," she said shakily. His closeness was beginning to make her tremble with the excitement that touching him always produced in her.

"From what I've read in the papers, you're a master of that way of life," he persisted.

His finger caressed the back of her neck as he held her to him, and a warm pleasant feeling was filling her.

"I suppose so." Her head tipped back so he could kiss her. She stared up at him from beneath the thick seductive curl of her lashes.

"I'm not sure this is the life for you," he said, "living in the country with a country doctor who has very little time off. I won't make much money."

His powerful body slowly forced her backward until she was pressed against a tall, gray tree trunk. He leaned against her in masculine possession. She had a curious floating feeling. It was suddenly so difficult to concentrate on what he was saying. She was noticing how his steamy breath mated with hers in the cold, evening air.

"I don't care about money," she murmured in a sensual whisper.

"Rich people always say that, honey," he murmured.

His lean muscular body was all that was real, and the strong hands that forced her softer shape to mold to the hard length of his male form. She gasped at the new intimacy of their tantalizing contact.

"Do they?" She scarcely knew what she said.

"Maybe money is something you take for granted...more than you know," Grant said as Abigail's arms wound around his neck with the deliberate purpose of drawing his mouth down to hers. "Maybe it's something you can't live without."

"Maybe," she muttered as his mouth covered hers in a blaze of enchantment. But it was Grant she felt she couldn't live without.

Desire quivered through her body, igniting a hundred fires whose heat seemed to turn her bones to hot fluid and her blood to liquid flame. His mouth hardened, seeking and demanding, ravishing. His caresses aroused her. His hand slid hotly up her arm and drew her arms tighter around his neck. Her fingertips played in the curling thickness of his auburn hair.

Her heart thrummed against her rib cage with a

deafening thunder, pulsing a wild pagan tempo. His hands were roaming, one of them curving, exploring the lush mounds of her stiff-tipped, soft breasts. Abigail trembled at this new intimacy, revelled in it.

Grant was driven by the same passionate force, but he was stronger than she. He released her lips, and she felt his ragged breath against her throat when he kissed her there.

"Abbie, we're wandering away from the subject of our discussion."

"Yes," she murmured. "Isn't it nice though?"

"Our conversation was boring you then?"

"This is definitely more interesting." She pursed her lips expectantly, and he lowered his mouth to graze them with a kiss.

"Wanton…" he accused, returning again to taste her parted lips.

She said nothing as he punished her mouth with plundering passion.

"You realize, of course, that I have absolutely no intention of marrying you," he said. His hand was still encircling her breast, cupping its lush ripeness. Her hips were still pinned against his, crushed by the thrusting size of his steel-hard thighs.

Nine generations of Bainbridges would have heard this statement and been appalled, but a very errant member of the tenth generation merely listened as sensual waves of longing washed through her.

"Of course..." she agreed.

"Under the circumstances, neither of us should make a commitment at this point," he went on.

She sighed. If only he would stop talking and thoroughly kiss her.

But he ignored the pouting temptation of her upturned lips, enticingly lush though they were.

"Maybe we need to see if our feelings can sustain themselves when faced with the realities of life," he said. "Maybe you really need all that Bainbridge hoopla more than you think. Maybe you'll get tired of playing house when the house doesn't have forty rooms and ten servants. You might not be ready to make a commitment."

"For a man with so many doubts, I'm beginning to wonder why you came after me today," she teased softly, her blue, sparkling eyes tilting coquettishly up at him from beneath her dark lashes.

From the smug complacence of her expression, he knew she expected a compliment, and the perverse side of his nature sprang to the force.

He grinned down at her. "Well...since you asked," he began. "Last night I was watching *The Graduate*."

"What does that silly old movie have to do with us?" she asked, puzzled.

"Everything, darling. Don't you see?"

"No, I don't see."

"I was drinking…rather heavily…and thinking of you," he said. "When Benjamen stormed down that aisle and grabbed his bride, I was into my seventh beer, and all I'd eaten was a TV dinner. As I watched him, I said to myself, 'What a fool! Who in the hell would do a fool thing like that?' But the idea seemed better and better to me the more I thought on it, and then I said, 'Why the hell not?' I guess I was swept away by the sentimental ending when Benjamen flew out of that church with his bride on his arm. You know what a sucker I am when it comes to Hollywood and happy endings."

"Do you mean if you hadn't been watching *The Graduate,* you wouldn't have…"

Her voice was tinged with desperation. His explanation had completely erased the look of smug complacence from her features. She had wanted a sensual compliment; she had expected a passionate avowal of his love, and instead he was giving her this…this bald truth that was so abysmally unflattering she almost wanted to cry. He'd decided to come after her when he was drunk and because of a ridiculous old movie and its maudlin ending! When she tried indignantly to push him away, he held her all the more tightly against himself, smiling down at her scowling face with the most infuriatingly perverse, roguish amusement.

"Let me finish at least before you unleash that hot temper of yours," he said. "Well, after the movie I went into the kitchen and made myself the strongest pot of black coffee you've ever seen. I took a long walk and drank at least five cups of coffee to sober up so I could drive into Pittsburgh. You see, even sober, I thought it was worth a chance—even if the odds were a million to one. All I had to lose was making an utter fool of myself in front of you and everybody who's anybody in Pittsburgh. But so what! None of them are impressed by the likes of me anyway! The only one I cared about was you. And if I couldn't have you, what did I care what you thought?"

"But you wouldn't have come…" She was sobbing and hating herself for it. She wanted to pound his chest, and he was laughing down at her. "…if you hadn't been watching that old movie?"

"Probably not," he admitted truthfully. He didn't say he'd been too stubborn and too proud to tell her. Nor did he flatter her wounded ego by telling her of the torment her absence had caused him. "But aren't you glad I watched it?" he goaded.

"No!" she stormed, trying to struggle and free herself from his powerful grasp.

"And just a minute ago you were all soft and

snuggly and coy,'' he whispered. "I'll bet I can make you glad...again.'' His hands wandered knowledgeably over her. He felt her quick intake of breath when they caressed her breasts. "I know I can.''

She was so outraged she couldn't speak, but despite her fury, her pulse was beating erratically in response to the intimate huskiness in his voice and the hard pressure of his hands and body gripping hers. Her legs felt shaky and weak. The soft, dark forest smelled sweet. A strange, compelling emotion suffused her.

"W-what are you going to do?'' she asked shakily.

"Don't you remember this place?'' he asked very softly, stroking the sensitive cord along her neck.

"No!'' She tried to twist her head away from the sensual touch of his fingers, but without success.

"This is where we made love...that special time.'' His hands roamed with indolent ease over her slender body, molding her with deliberate expertise to his granite length.

"It is!'' Her voice was oddly squeaky, and she didn't recognize it as her own.

How different it had been in summer, when hummingbirds and bees had hovered among the soft sweet-smelling rose blossoms that perfumed the air, when the lush grasses had been pearled with lustrous dewdrops, when wild columbine had bloomed. Or had her imagination merely painted that magic time with poetic beauty?

"I'm going to make love to you, Abbie," he whispered as his lips began intimately to trace the delicate line of her jaw. "And you're going to make love to me."

"This is crazy, Grant! You just admitted that you wouldn't have come after me if you hadn't been watching that silly old movie! And even then...you almost didn't make it on time!" As she protested, her mouth parted in anticipation of his kiss. Her soft body arched against the hardness of his.

"But I did come. Always read the bottom line, Abbie," he murmured softly, and she caught the intoxicating flavor of his breath. His lips hovered an inch above hers without possessing her mouth.

Why could he so easily make her feel as if she were hanging on an emotional cliff? She wanted to be furious, but she couldn't be, because he no longer willed it. A minute ago he'd deliberately manipulated her into anger, and now he was just as deliberately manipulating her out of it, and before she was ready to abandon the rather dubious joy of her feminine outrage.

His hands burned over her skin, arousing her body to match the fever of his.

Flames of desire leaped and soared around the

lovers, melting them into one. They trembled with their hunger for one another.

Grant's fingers combed through her hair, smoothing wayward tendrils away from her face. She felt his hand beneath her chin, exerting a faint pressure, tilting her mouth toward his. Through the thick curl of her half-closed lashes, Abigail observed him looking down at her; her heart skittered as she noted his avid gaze dwelling upon her lips.

"You're beautiful," he murmured, pulling her closer against his warm body. "Dangerously beautiful." His mouth twisted cynically. "You know what you do to a man, and you don't care." His breath was a warm caress against her cheek. "Even if it destroys me, I can't fight you any longer."

She didn't want to succumb to the passion in his voice, but she couldn't stop herself. As his lips lowered to hers she could do nothing but submit to their fierce possession. The instant his hot mouth covered hers, the deepening intimacy of his kiss enflamed the passionate core within her. Waves of responsive desire spread their yielding fire through every part of her being. A million stars exploded; a thousand rockets roared and blazed. With trembling rapture she swayed against the solid muscle of his chest, her hands curving around his neck in complete abandon.

He was kissing her everywhere, his hunger for her insatiable. His hands moved down her spine, tracing the curve of her waist and hips, shaping her female form to the hardness of his aroused body. Abigail pressed closer, her pulse roaring in her breast, while her emotions whirled at the exquisite torture of his crushing embrace. She felt his tongue thrust inside the honeyed depths of her mouth, twirling in sensual exploration against the soft hot inner walls.

She moaned in sheer ecstasy from the deepest part of her soul. "Oh…Grant…"

She felt his fingers unbutton her jacket; it slid down her body into a heap near her feet. So hotly stirred was she from his kisses and the leaping white-hot flames of her desire that she scarcely noticed the chilled air against her naked skin as he pushed her thin sweater above her breasts.

He removed his mouth from her tingling flesh.

"Abbie?"

"Hmm?" Her skin seemed to burn everywhere he'd kissed her, everywhere his hands had touched her. She wanted him. The completeness of her intimate longing frightened her, but she could do nothing but wish for the immediate consummation of her need.

She heard his low resonant drawl through the haze of her desire.

"Are you glad, Abbie?" he asked.

"Glad?" She felt so thoroughly confused, so

dazed she could scarcely comprehend him, much less answer.

"That I came?" he persisted devilishly.

She caught his meaning, remembering that he'd made her glad he'd watched *The Graduate* and come after her. Despite her own passion, a slow, perverse smile curved her lips. "In a way," she murmured. "I suppose…I'm glad." She reached up and nibbled at the bottom of his earlobe in a deliberately tantalizing fashion.

"What do you mean—in a way?" he asked, a bit of the usual arrogance in his deep tone absent.

"Every time we get together it's so exciting, so dangerously explosive," she whispered teasingly. "Like oxygen and flame or a spark and gasoline. The fire between us always gets out of hand."

"It does, doesn't it," he agreed huskily. The tone of his voice sent a tremor through her limbs.

"Of course it's a purely physical thing, this combustion between us," she said.

"That's what I keep telling myself," he agreed.

"And maybe it's time we let all those fires burn themselves out."

"Do you really think they will?"

"I don't know, Grant. But won't it be fun finding out?"

She smiled as his arms tightened fiercely about her and drew her down upon a bed of soft leaves and high grasses. A tiny cry of surrender escaped her lips as his mouth closed over hers with passionate ardency, his tongue moving inside to mate with hers.

A wild, sublime enchantment wrapped them like the hot, dark power of a witch's spell. They were lovers as they had been lovers before, so long ago, in a complete and utter coming together that fused their bodies, their minds, and their souls.

Because of the fire they were determined to let burn out, Abigail and Grant began their life together with even more of the usual enthusiasm of new couples, as well as with more doubts. The first person they took into their confidence was Aunt Peggy, for in spite of the fact that Abigail was a modern girl, she was still a Bainbridge, born and bred. This prevented her from simply moving in with Grant. Grant teased her unmercifully about being a hypocrite, but to no avail.

"I simply can't live with a man I'm not married to—not even you!" she stated passionately every time he brought up her moving in with him.

"There's the Bainbridge in you coming out," he chuckled maddeningly. "You just can't do without the luxury of living in a mansion," he accused lightly on more than one occasion.

She'd burst out laughing the first time he said it.

"Luxury? At Aunt Peggy's? The place is a fifty-room kennel, not a mansion! I have to play nurse-maid to a menagerie of guinea pigs, cats, dogs, parrots and even a pet skunk. You know Aunt Peggy hates maids and mows the five acres near the house herself."

"I'd forgotten all those small details."

"Rather conveniently."

Aunt Peggy had relented at the very last minute and actually attended Abigail's wedding. She was delighted at the events that had transpired and gave the lovers her full support.

"I really would make it a point to go to more weddings, Abigail dear, if they were all as exciting as yours, despite the difficulties of leaving the animals."

From her possessive perch on her mistress's ample lap, Fuzzy flattened her ears at this remark and looked quite sulky. She began swishing her white tail irritably. It looked like a giant ostentatious feather waving disdainfully back and forth. The other cats, and there were at least eight of them in the blue, sun-dappled kitchen at the time, chose that moment to get into a quick squabble amongst themselves as Roar, Aunt Peggy's German shepherd, leaped into the room through the animal door and stalked warily across the striped throw rugs.

"Oh dear! You see, Abigail, how upset the poor

things became when I threaten to leave?'' Aunt Peggy stood up with the aristocratic Fuzzy still in her arms. The cat's white ears flattened against her skull again as she observed Roar from the safety of her mistress's arms. Aunt Peggy shushed her nervous pets with motherly gestures and cooing words that she was sure they understand as plainly as meows or barks. ''There, there, darlings, Mother won't leave you to go to any silly old weddings.'' To an assorted garble of mews and loud barks: ''Of course not, darlings. Quite! Quite! Ridiculous!''

There were certain advantages to living with her aunt that outweighed the disadvantages. Abigail loved her aunt's vast cedar-shingled house, because she had many pleasant childhood memories associated with it. When she walked about the grounds in the chill twilight hours before supper, she took the worn path that skirted the edge of the gleaming leaf-strewn pond. She always wandered to the playhouse that stood on the opposite bank where she had once played during long summer afternoons. The playhouse was a replica in miniature of Joslynn, with duplicate soaring chimneys and jutting wings. Viewed from across the lake, the main house was magnificent, and Abigail was reminded that houses and estates like Joslynn belonged to another, grander age. Joslynn had been her mother's family's summer house.

Grant was away working so much of the time that Abigail might have grown lonely in the cottage without enough to do and without her feisty aunt's companionship. At her aunt's there were animals to be fed and spoiled, an enormous house that needed keeping. Too, her aunt immediately proved helpful in solving a problem that had been tormenting Abigail—what to do with the Harrison diamond.

"I can't face Harold or Mother yet," Abigail explained one day as she and Aunt Peggy were sweeping at least ten years' worth of cobwebs out of the corners of her porch. "But I want to write Harold a letter and explain. I'm afraid I've hurt him and humiliated him, and if I'd been honest with him in the first place, I could have avoided doing that. And I feel I have to return his ring immediately, before something happens to it. I can't take it off because I'm so afraid I'll lose it, and I can't wear it because I can't stand to! Grant doesn't seem to think the ring is all that important."

"Of course, it's important to get rid of it at once, and I'll take it back. I'll take your letter to Harold," Aunt Peggy said briskly, pausing to rest on her broom handle. "I'll give them to Rosalind or to that pompous old fool of a butler who scarcely speaks to me if she won't receive me herself."

"She'll receive you."

"Of course she will. How else will she let us know of her suffering at our hands?"

"None of this is your fault, Aunt Peggy. She certainly can't blame you."

"Oh, but she can. She's been blaming me for everything for years! But I don't care in the least. I've never minded being the burr beneath all those fancy silk and satin coverlets of hers. But I think Rosalind will see me, because she's always been insatiably curious beneath that armor of propriety. I'm certain she's simply popping to know what's going on, for all that she'll be playing the indignantly wronged martyr to the hilt. Why, I'll bet she's having the time of her life! Didn't I tell you that was the most exciting wedding I've ever been to? And she engineered it. For all we know, she's basking in glory!"

"Somehow I doubt Mother sees it that way."

"Anything's possible," Aunt Peggy replied tartly. "Else what do you suppose the two of us are doing out here this very minute, swabbing at cobwebs I've lived quite amicably with for a quarter of a century when neither of us gives a flip for housework?"

Abigail chuckled. "You've got a point."

"Let's let the spiders have the porch, Abigail dear. Why don't we stop this nonsense and have a cup of tea. Besides, we're upsetting my poor darlings by staying out here and ignoring them."

Aunt Peggy and Abigail never did get back to their abandoned brooms and cobwebs.

And so Aunt Peggy drove to Pittsburgh with the ring and a long, tear-splotched letter for Harold, leaving Abigail a lengthy list concerning the idiosyncrasies of her darlings and specific instructions for their care—who was to have heartworm pills, who was to have vitamin tablets and how many, who ate what brand of canned food, who had to eat on the ledge apart from the others, and who had to have liver bits especially pan fried for him.

When Abigail had completed these chores with the animals, she took out a giant canvas and set it up on an easel she had brought from her studio. She chose a sun porch where sunlight sifted through beveled glass windows until early afternoon. The animals watched her with unfeigned curiosity and settled themselves about the room atop throw rugs and on stuffed couches to have an unobscured view of this new excitement. It was the first of many days Abigail was to spend painting before her furry audience—really painting. Not the dot pictures, but an attempt at what she'd really wanted to do for a long time.

The work proved terribly difficult, and she was filled with self-doubts at the slow progress of her work, at its failure to live up to her preliminary vision. But Grant and Aunt Peggy encouraged her, and somehow despite the heartache and difficulty of it all, she found herself, paintbrush in hand, standing before the great splotched canvas with her visiting army of fur balls encamped about her early every morning. And she remained later every afternoon.

During this time, she felt her life was in limbo. Grant worked terribly hard; there were some evenings when she didn't even see him at all. Sometimes he remained at the hospital for whole weekends, and the time they had together was too brief and precious to spend driving into Pittsburgh to the glamorous restaurants or plays she had enjoyed with Harold. She was learning again how to savor the simple pleasures of life, as she'd learned so long ago during the glorious summer she'd spent with her aunt.

In the evenings Abigail and Grant took short walks in the forest, returning to the cottage every fifteen minutes to check his phone when he was on call. They gathered firewood and built enormous fires that roared and crackled while they popped golden popcorn and roasted countless marshmallows, feeding each other these delicacies, then licking each other's sticky fingers. They spoke of what they had done in each other's absence—she of her painting and the antics of Aunt Peggy's animals, he of his patients and their problems.

Abigail looked forward most of all to the inevitable passion that overtook them so spontaneously. They could be enjoying the beauty of the creek splashing against the rocks beneath the trees or the beautiful wonder of a new snow when suddenly Grant would take her in his arms. Once she'd been cooking his dinner at the stove, and he'd been overcome by the beauty of her at the task.

He'd swept her against his hard body, and dinner had been forgotten for a very long time.

Everything would have been perfect were it not for their unresolved doubts concerning the past— and Abigail's secret concerning the existence of their son, Michael.

Sometimes in the middle of the night when Grant had left her to return to his cottage or to make a house call and Abigail lay in her bed trying to sleep, she yearned so deeply for Michael it was like a physical wound. She wanted to tell Grant that they had a precious son, but she knew that that would inevitably lead to a discussion of all the hurts in the past as well as an open confrontation with Rosalind. And Abigail wasn't sure their new relationship was strong enough to withstand these pressures.

Long ago Grant had left her pregnant and afraid, and she'd stood alone against Rosalind. Was it any wonder that she couldn't be sure of his love, no matter how wonderfully true it seemed?

And so the crisp fall days gave way to winter without either of them attempting to deepen the commitment to the other. They were both afraid.

Ten

"**A**bbie, I'm asking you to marry me."

A log crackled, sending a burst of sputtering sparks upward. Otherwise the cottage was silent, and Grant's words pounded through Abigail like startling shafts of pain.

Snowflakes were drifting lazily out of a leaden sky; soon it would be pitch dark outside, except for the tiny bulb Grant had left switched on out on the porch. Inside, the cottage was snug and warm from the roaring fire Grant had built in the grate; the kitchen was awash with the delicious aromas of baking chicken and fresh steaming vegetables.

But despite the golden glow of the cottage and

the ruddy warmth of the fire, a terrible pain locked itself like a tight band of steel around the soft tissue of Abigail's heart. It was incredible that Grant could be saying the words she'd dreamed of him saying for eight long years and that those words merely compounded her misery.

She clutched the chilled windowsill, staring unseeingly out the window. She wanted to be anywhere, anywhere but here with him. At long last she had come face-to-face with all the realities that both of them had put off for the past ten weeks. And she was afraid, afraid as she'd never been before, for she knew that facing these realities brought with it the terrible risk of losing Grant forever.

Oh, they had already faced some realities. Her painting was a miserable failure, but she had learned a lot in the process of working on it. She did miss the excitement of living in a city rather more than she'd thought she would, and she found it difficult being tied down by the neverending responsibility of Grant's practice. She'd discovered as well that she got so bored at times in the country that she thought she'd go mad from the silence, from the vast, endless stillnesses, from the distances separating her from other human beings. And winter had scarcely begun! She had no friends other than Grant and Aunt Peggy, and she was terribly lonely for Michael. There was the unresolved conflict with her

family, and this disturbed her far more than she was
willing to admit. All of these things she'd tried to
keep from Grant, but her unhappiness had crept into
their relationship despite her attempts to prevent it.
As she stared out the window, she was thinking of
these things, determining to improve her attitude if
she couldn't change the circumstances.

She felt Grant's warmth even before his arms slid
around her waist, crushing her against his muscular
chest. As always, just his touch sent her heart ca-
reening and her spirits lifting. Her fingers closed
over his strong hands. The good thing in her life
was simply having him, being with him, sharing her
life with him. And despite the everyday realities, the
magic in their relationship was stronger than ever.

She felt his hands stroking her hair, and suddenly
she was crying, both because it was so wonderful to
be in his arms and so terrible to think of losing this
closeness with him that she so treasured.

"Abbie, Abbie, what is it? You haven't said a
word! Don't you want to marry me?" he murmured
softly against the thick, sweet-scented, flowing
golden coils cascading about her shoulders.

There, he'd repeated his question, restating his desire to make the commitment to her that he hadn't
been able to make eight years before. And this rep-
etition merely brought soul-wrenching sobs that

caught at his heart because he didn't understand the emotion that overpowered her.

"Yes…yes…I do…if you really mean it," she gasped in shuddering breaths against his powerful warm shoulder.

"Of course, I mean it, but I don't understand your mood tonight."

Of course he couldn't understand her mood, she thought dismally.

"There are so many things we have to talk about…before we can decide whether to marry," she managed weakly.

"I thought we'd been talking for ten weeks," he murmured in a very logical, male tone, "among other things…" His voice was suddenly silkily suggestive, recalling visions of their bodies entwined before the fireplace while music from the stereo swirled about, caressing them with a sensual blanket of sound. "I know living out here, away from everything you're used to, hasn't been as easy for you as you thought it would be. But I think you're adjusting amazingly well. It's going to take some time, but I think we can make it."

"We need to talk about the…past," she said darkly.

She felt him tense. She knew that the past disturbed him more than he ever admitted. But when he spoke, he deliberately kept his voice calm.

"Honey, I thought we'd agreed to forget the past, to start over. And if it's upsetting you this much, I see no point in going into irrelevant history. It hurt, but it's over. You've grown up since then."

His voice was deep and soothing, but she was thinking of his words. He still blamed her for what had happened, and a vague resentment stirred in her. He had left her, wanting no part of their child, and as a result he didn't know about Michael. He didn't know that Rosalind had lied about the miscarriage. Abigail knew he wouldn't have said what he'd said, had he known.

It wasn't going to be easy to tell him now, after so many years. She couldn't imagine how he would react. He hadn't wanted a child then.

She shivered, her unreasoning fear building as she struggled to find the words to explain a son he didn't know he had. It hurt so to remember that time when she'd been so alone that it seemed the whole world had turned against her. She'd had to fight everyone for her child.

Weakly she sagged against him, wanting to remember the feel of his strong arms about her. She was searingly aware of those arms tightly wrapping her body against his.

"Are you all right now?" he asked gently as he caressed her cheek with his hand.

"I know you think I'm silly," she murmured. But you won't in a minute, her worried mind nagged.

"No, I don't," he said ever so gently.

It was several minutes before Abigail reluctantly unwound Grant arms from her waist. Her legs felt weak and shaky, but she could stand without his support.

"I think I'm okay now," she said, keeping her eyes lowered as she moved away from the window toward the fire, away from him.

"We don't have to talk about the past now," he said. "Frankly, I don't think you're up to the discussion."

"Yes, I am." Oh, where to begin? Grant, there's a little something I neglected to tell you. He's seven, and his hair's exactly the shade of yours... For an instant his darkly handsome face blurred and swam, then she brushed at her eyes and her vision cleared.

For a long time she just stared at him in painful silence. The words wouldn't come.

"You might as well begin," he prodded.

"I suppose so." She trembled. "Grant, I hope you'll be able to understand why I didn't tell you this before."

"Of course, I'll understand," he said easily, leaning his great body negligently against the wall by the window.

She plunged bravely in. "When Mother told you

eight years ago that I had a miscarriage, she…well, she wasn't telling you the truth.''

The negligent ease of his great body was instantly gone, and the air that separated them was charged with a new and profound tension. Grant stared at her with the blank look of someone who had unexpectedly been socked in the gut and was momentarily too stunned even to realize he'd received a blow. He turned absolutely white; his eyes were like black coals glimmering darkly against his skin. His gaze never left her face.

Her low voice continued shakily in the too-still cottage.

''Grant, Mother only said that to make things easier…for everyone. There seemed no reason for you to be involved, since you were so against the baby.''

''What are you saying?'' he rasped, finding his voice at last, though it didn't sound at all like his own.

''Th-that I went on and had the baby. Oh, I know you didn't want it, but you see I couldn't let you make that decision. I wanted our son, in spite of what you had done.''

''Our son!'' The two words were an explosion.

In one fluid movement Grant was beside her, towering like an angry dark giant above her, his fierce eyes glittering in his cold, gray face. She felt the painful imprint of his fingers digging into the flesh of her arms. It was the first time he'd ever touched her roughly, and a terrifying tremor shuddered through her as he yanked her against himself, staring down at her as though he didn't recognize her. She looked fearfully up into his glowering features.

He was a violent stranger she didn't know, not the tender man she loved. She saw a muscle twitch along his tightly clenched jaw, and she knew he was barely holding the force of his temper in check. His fury terrified her, and she thought that in that moment he surely hated her.

His mind was a savage turmoil. Not only had she left him eight years ago, but she'd taken his baby from him as well.

"You and your mother kept my son from me... for eight damned years!" His low voice was ominously soft.

"What choice did I have?" she implored.

He stared harshly down at her as though he considered her words those of an insane person. When he spoke it was through gritted teeth.

"What choice?" he snapped impatiently. "You damned stupid little fool! What choice? And I thought I could forgive you anything. Well, I can't, Abigail. Not this! Never this!"

Fear clutched her heart with icy, clawing fingers. She felt as though she were suffocating, dying. This cold implacable stranger felt no love for her. She'd lost him—his love, everything that mattered to her, and without Grant's love she felt unbearably alienated and alone. Suddenly desperate to make him understand, she braved his terrifying wrath.

"Grant...I...if you'd only listen to me, I could explain—"

"Don't speak to me!" he yelled down at her, his sharp words brutally cutting off her soft, trembling attempt at explanation. "I don't want to hear your voice—all sweetness and innocence. How are you capable of such blind, monstrous selfishness?"

"Me?" She stared up at him, some of her own hurt dissolving at the injustice of this accusation. She remembered the terrible loneliness of his desertion. She'd been hardly more than a child. Suddenly she was growing angry herself.

"Where is he?" Grant demanded savagely, shaking her so that the golden waves of her hair showered loosely about her shoulders, its softness bouncing upon his bronzed hands. "What did you do with my son? Did you give him away to strangers—to some suitable adoption agency that knows how to suitably dispose of inconvenient bastards like...like our son?"

How could he even think her capable of such a horrifying thing? She stared up at him in stupefied agony.

His grip cruelly bruised the flesh of her arms.

"Answer me!" he thundered. "What did you do with my son?"

"My sister, Lisa, took him...until she and her husband were killed. Mother has custody of Michael now...until I marry."

"Michael..." Deep relief washed through Grant. His son was not lost to him forever. For just an instant he forgot his anger toward Abigail in the wonder of learning his son's name and in the relief that his son had not been given to strangers and lost to him forever. "Michael was my father's name. Did you name him...after my father?"

"Yes."

"What's he... What's Michael like?"

"He's like you."

"Tell me about this custody arrangement," Grant said grimly, the force of his anger once more upon him.

"When she died, my sister gave Mother temporary custody of Michael until I married. That's all. That's one reason I was marrying Harold, you see, to give Michael a home and a father... I wanted to be his mother...at last...to have him live with me."

"How admirably noble of you." There was a jeering element in Grant's deep tone. "Forgive me if it's difficult for me to forget the insignificant fact that Harrison is so abominably rich and that, by giving Michael such a father, you were robbing me of my son as well as setting yourself up to live rather splendidly.''

"Harold's money never mattered to me.''

Grant laughed harshly. "I'll bet! Do you know how it makes me feel that you could marry him? That you were going to give him my son? If I hadn't come after you on your wedding day, all that would be an accomplished fact right now!''

"But you didn't want Michael, Grant! All your self-righteous anger at this point is a little difficult for me to endure.''

She struggled to pull away from him, but he effortlessly tightened his grasp upon her shoulders, little caring if he hurt her.

He stared down at her in disbelief. "How the hell can you say I didn't want my own son—when I didn't even know he existed?''

"But when Mother told you I was pregnant, you—''

"Rosalind never told me a damned thing, and you know it!''

Abigail stared up at him, completely at a loss for words. "You know she did, Grant! She did!''

Some of the anger went out of him as he gazed at Abigail's beautiful troubled face, at the tears glimmering at the corners of her eyes. Her beautiful face was tilted up toward his, and he saw all the agony and regret and doubt written upon it as well as her love for him.

Had Rosalind lied to them both? he wondered. But even as this new hope flickered in his mind, he stamped it out with vicious roughness. He was a fool to so desperately want to believe that Rosalind was wholly to blame, and not his beloved Abigail, for keeping the knowledge of his son from him.

"No, Abbie, she didn't," he said quietly. "But neither did you."

"But I thought she—"

"You could have told me yourself."

"But she sent me away, and I didn't know where you were."

"Rosalind knew where to reach me."

Grant's fingers were digging into her arms, but Abigail was too numb to feel the pain. She searched his grave face for the answers she so desperately needed, for the truths that eluded her.

Was he lying—because it now sat more comfortably on his conscience to do so? Or had her mother lied all those years ago? But Rosalind Bainbridge never lied, and young men caught with the inconvenient responsibilities of unwanted fatherhood did.

Abigail had lived the last eight years of her life upon the foundation of his betrayal. It was impossible that she could have been wrong about him, wasn't it? Yet some part of her was struggling desperately to believe in him, to believe in his love and its fidelity. But she couldn't. For eight years she'd deliberately stamped out the natural romanticism of her nature, and she was incapable of instantly resurrecting it. Now, even though his fury and his defense of himself raised a reasonable doubt in her mind, she was too conditioned by the cynical truths she'd taught herself to believe to trust him. Besides that, and perhaps more importantly, she was afraid to believe him. For if she believed him, if she found she'd been wrong all those years, the pain and the loss for those wasted years would have to be faced. She would hate herself for doubting his love and for betraying him.

At last she said, "Oh, Grant, what are we going to do about this? I feel so mixed up! I don't know what to believe anymore! I don't know which way to turn! I don't know what to do!"

In the deadliest of tones he said, "My dear, it's very simple really. You're going to marry me!" At her look of total confusion, he added, "Whether you want to or not, because I want my son. And that's the easiest way I know to get him."

"B-but…you don't want to marry me now. I can feel your dislike. You—"

"My feelings for you have nothing to do with any of this," he grated harshly. "I want my son, and you're going to give him to me."

"Grant...I can't...I won't let you do this to us."

"You don't have a choice. Say you'll marry me!" His fingers were clenched about her slim shoulders as he clamped her against his body. She felt every hard muscle in his body as her soft form rested unresistingly against his. "Say it, damn you!"

She cringed inwardly at the malevolence in his eyes, at the smoldering anger in his voice.

"And I thought you wanted to marry me," he jeered.

"I do," she said weakly. "But not like this. Never like this."

"If you don't, I'll fight you every inch of the way for custody of my son."

She saw savage pain in his expression as well as bleak hopelessness in his stance, and she knew suddenly how much she'd hurt him by denying him Michael. If she didn't marry him, she knew it would be practically impossible for him to obtain Michael. Though she sensed an utterly ruthless determination to bend her to his will building in him, that wasn't what moved her to agree to his terrible proposal.

She couldn't, she wouldn't fight him, for she couldn't bear to see him go up against the might of the Bainbridge wealth and their lawyers—and lose. She knew what it was to fight her mother. Grant wouldn't have a chance of getting his son unless she married him.

"All right, Grant," she mumbled numbly. "I'll marry you. But I doubt if any of us will find happiness—marrying for these reasons."

"I'm not looking for happiness any longer. The possibility of that was over the minute I found out you deliberately kept Michael from me all these years, that you believed I wasn't good enough to be the father of my own son." Every fiber of his being rippled with violence and tension.

With that he stormed out of the cottage into the whirling snow, leaving her the most painful solitude she'd ever experienced.

She stifled a sob. She was glad he was gone; she felt too ashamed to face him after all the hurt she'd brought him.

Eleven

Abigail scarcely saw Grant until the marriage ceremony that he arranged in the village a week later. She tried to tell herself that she didn't care, that she was the one who had been wronged, not he. Hadn't he left her pregnant and been indifferent to her fate? But if that was so, why was he acting so violently hurt now, so stubbornly angry?

No one was invited to the brief service, not even Aunt Peggy. Grant wouldn't allow it. Abigail wondered if he was ashamed to be marrying her. Two shabbily dressed strangers off the street were the only witnesses.

Grant stood stiffly beside her in a poorly heated,

drab little beige office behind the sanctuary of the quaint little church. Abigail's only demand had been that they be married in a church with a minister to perform the ceremony. When she'd said she wanted to be married in a church, she'd never thought the wedding would be performed in this horrible little room, with these close walls that induced a suffocating feeling of claustrophobia. As she gazed around the room, she knew that she would remember every minute detail for the rest of her life—the shapes of the stains on the tattered brown carpet, the chipped paint flaking off the moldings in egg-shell curls, the drafts seeping beneath the door jamb and chilling her ankles, the terrible whistling of the wind through the naked trees outside.

During the ceremony Grant stood rigidly beside her slight trembling form, careful that his body did not accidentally touch hers. Nor did he look at her. He spoke his vows coldly, each word clipped and precise, cutting the silence in the small room like knife blades.

Beside her, he seemed a tall bronzed giant clad in his navy wool suit. He showed no shred of emotion, and a fierce pain swelled in Abigail's heart as the ceremony seemed to drag on and on. When at last they were pronounced man and wife, Grant turned toward her for the first time, and the deep bitterness in his gaze as he looked down at her made her shudder with hurt. For an instant his handsomely carved features were dark with some indefinable emotion, then he tore his eyes from her face and stared past her as if it were preferable to stare at nothing than at her.

Her pulse beat with desperate, painful thuds. Oh, why couldn't he forgive her? Why must he be so determined to hate her? Was his love gone forever? Would he ever be able to forget what she had done? Couldn't he see that he hadn't been blameless and that she had forgiven him?

All these questions whirled in her troubled mind, battering her so painfully that suddenly she couldn't stand the agony of his nearness, for she was constantly reminded of his cold dislike for her. She would have rushed from him then out into the bleak, snowy world, away from this mockery of marriage he was inflicting upon them both. But he caught her in his arms and held her tightly against him, his closeness making her terribly aware of the dangerous virility that lurked just beneath the surface of his civilized veneer. His arms about her waist were powerful, and she swayed against him. His mouth came down and brushed hers coolly, without passion, without the love or tenderness that she so longed for. Quick tears dampened her eyelids, but she fought them. He released her only when he felt her submit to the brutal domination of his embrace and his kiss, when he felt the tension drain from her body and with it her strength to flee him.

On the way back to the cottage, Grant drove without speaking. His deliberate silence was grating Abigail's nerves raw, but she didn't dare say anything herself. She saw the buildings on the outskirts of the village rush past in a blur of colors against the snow as the car sped out toward the darkness of the forest. The blinking lights of the familiar little motel at the edge of the village came into view. Suddenly, without warning, Grant turned the Valiant sharply into the gravel drive that wound to the motel set back within the shadows of the trees.

Abigail was thrown roughly against his hard body, and she felt the ripple of every taut muscle beneath his tailored suit. She jerked herself quickly away, trying to freeze her involuntary response to his virile body. "What are you doing?" she demanded nervously, looking out at the individual squat cabins in alarm.

He braked in front of the cabin that was farthest from the office. In his hand a brass motel key glittered. Obviously he'd made prior arrangements that he hadn't bothered to inform her about.

"It's our wedding night, remember?" He said it so coldly that a terrible chill shivered through her, a chill that had nothing to do with the snow beginning to filter downward or with the cold air sifting inside the car now that the engine heater was off.

"But why stop here?" Her question was brief. The silence that followed it was so pregnant with embarrassment that she turned bright red when his dark, gleaming eyes roved over her.

"Isn't it obvious?" he asked with the sardonic lift of a black brow. Arrogance outlined the hard lines of his face as he reached for her and pulled her soft body against his own that was as lean and hard and tough as a pirate's. "Why not?" he muttered.

She tried to twist away, but the steel circle of his arms wrapped her tightly against him. The heat of him was like a furnace warming her.

"It's my conjugal right now," he taunted. One of his hands moved intimately down her throat, slowly moving lower, molding and shaping itself to the warm curves of her body, lingering upon her breast with bold, male insolence. "I'm only taking what is legally mine," he murmured with a quick, white smile that never reached his eyes.

The warmth of his breath against her forehead, the clean, tantalizingly masculine scent of him, the hard feel of him, his hand cupping her breast with masculine possessiveness—all these things combined and rocked her senses.

"Yes, but why…when you feel so….so…" she

struggled breathlessly. "When you don't want me?" she managed at last.

"I never said I didn't want you," he muttered fiercely. "If only I didn't! If only I could rid myself of thinking of you, of wanting you…" She felt the power of him, the latent sensuality, the wild passion that not even his most determined control could fully curb. And some traitorous part of her leaped in response. She felt hot and cold and breathless…and suddenly very desperate.

His hot mouth closed cruelly over hers even as she twisted and struggled frantically to evade his lips. Pushing against him, she felt the iron hardness of his muscles. Every part of him was hard, and her soft body had to yield to accommodate his.

His kiss deepened, and he forced her lips apart to accept the sensual exploration of his tongue. He wanted to taste her, to invade her body with his maleness. He felt that his needs were consuming him.

Slowly her strength to fight was leaving her. She couldn't resist his fierce, relentless passion. The fingers of one hand were twined through the darkness of his hair where it curled against his collar. She felt dizzily weak, lost, as she gave into a will that was stronger than her own. Her other hand was twisting the buttons of his shirt. He was so hot, so deli-

ciously, so wantonly hot, like a burning fire in a
world that was cold and alien and silent.

As her resistance ebbed, so did his violent determination to make her submit. He withdrew his
mouth from hers slowly, as though with great reluctance, and she felt his hot breath whisper raggedly
across her cheek.

"I think we'd better go inside, don't you?" he
mocked, staring down at the unbuttoned bodice of
her silk dress, at her pink-tipped breasts pushing
against the bristly hairs of his own darkly tanned
chest.

Her eyes flew in horror to his muscular body as
well as to her own. In her passion she had done
that—ripped his shirt apart so that she could touch
him with her hands and with other parts of her body
as well.

"We should stop now," she murmured, knowing
full well that this argument was useless. "You don't
love me—not anymore."

"To hell with love." His lips twisted cynically.
"My feelings have nothing to do with this. We have
to consummate the marriage, don't we, my love? Or
should I say 'my wife'?"

He said this last so bitterly that she cringed.

She scarcely heard his low voice continue. "I
don't intend to give Rosalind even a single round of
ammunition to fight her battle against me. So you

see, I have to make love to you, sweet, whether or not I want to.'' There was a bitter, trapped look in his expression.

Again she felt chilled, this time both because of his harsh expression and the utter ruthlessness in his low tone.

''Oh, Grant, please! Don't…don't do this.''

He ignored her pleading, deliberately stamping out the damnable weakness in himself that always made him want to protect her. ''I don't like it any better than you,'' he hurled, a forbidding light burning in the frightening black depths of his eyes as he flung his door open.

She watched him helplessly, but he wasn't looking at her any longer. He'd turned to step out into the sifting snowflakes. His profile was as hard and unyielding as chiseled granite.

''I'll go around and open your door,'' he said curtly.

Hot tears stung her eyelids as she watched his tall, broad-shouldered form stride swiftly around the hood of the Valiant. Her door snapped open with the suddenness of a trap door, and his hand took hers forcefully in his.

The tiny cabin was as cold as ice. Abigail was overwhelmingly aware of Grant's every movement as he switched on the heater. She stood stiffly at the door. When he had finished, he gave her a long, hard look, his anger so tightly leashed that she felt frightened. This room seemed so isolated; she'd never felt more terribly alone with him. For some reason she began to tremble.

He glanced toward the lumpy little double bed in the center of the room and then back at her with a bold gaze that made her flush crimson.

If only he would take her in his arms, the awful little room wouldn't seem so awful.

"Take off your clothes," he commanded brusquely, his brown hand going to his collar and loosening his maroon tie, savagely jerking the knot so that the two ends dangled freely against his chest. He began unbuttoning his shirt, and she watched weakly as a strip of lean torso was revealed.

He shrugged out of his navy coat and light blue shirt and tossed them carelessly onto a nearby chair. Abigail watched the play of his muscles; his shoulders and chest gleamed like hard, rippling copper. With the shedding of these clothes, he seemed to shed the civilized aura of the doctor he was and become a primitive male with primitive instincts.

His brown hand unsnapped the buckle of his belt. Abigail's heart thudded in her throat as she watched him.

Suddenly he glanced toward her frozen form in contempt. "Well, what are you waiting for?"

His voice was so hard and cold, new tears sprang

behind her eyelids. "I—I can't..." she murmured, too distraught to say more.

There was no softening in him even at the sight of her too-bright eyes. Grant moved silently toward her, his body pagan and splendid and as fluidly graceful as that of a great dark panther. His black eyes ripped away blue silk and roamed over every female curve with deliberate insolence. When he reached her, he circled her waist roughly with his hard arms, drawing her hips tightly against his, flattening her breasts against his muscular chest.

She was instantly, sharply aware of his maleness. She pushed ineffectually against the taut muscles of his chest and shoulders. The hard feel of his naked chest beneath her quivering fingertips ignited a tiny, raw, sensual flame deep within her. Shakily she drew a deep, quick breath, inwardly battling against this treacherous arousal of her senses.

"I can see I'll have to undress you myself," he taunted. When she shrank from him, his expression grew even more harsh. "But I don't mind. In fact, I'll enjoy it."

She stiffened as she felt his hand slide over her shoulder. His warm fingers impatiently jerked the silken bow at her neck. For a long moment he held the ends with his strong, hard hands, staring at her so possessively she grew breathless. Then he wound the ends around his fists, using them to capture her, pulling her even closer to him before he let the gauzy streamers flutter once more against her breasts.

He undid the first button at her throat and then the second. She was keenly aware of the heat of his fingers against her skin, of their deliberate movements as he unfastened each button until he'd stripped her to the waist, just as she was aware of his ruthless gaze devouring the voluptuous charms of her lush curves. A solitary tear trickled down her cheek.

He knew how to look at a woman, how to touch a woman, how to hold a woman so that her only awareness was of him.

He pushed her dress over her hips, touching her intimately as he did so. She felt as hot as flame, as wild as a mountain storm roaring through the forest in the night. He felt her shiver every time he lingeringly touched her thighs, and his white smile was mocking and cynical when she gasped.

Oh, he knew her too well! He knew how to tease, to tantalize until all her pride was gone and all that remained was her passionate need. She didn't want to feel this way!

"Let me go! Please, Grant, don't do this,' she begged shakily in a last ditch plea for his mercy.

But he was not in a merciful mood. Harsh, low laughter met this plea, and he seemed even more fiercely urgent than before. Her dress and undergarments were stripped brutally away and she stood naked before him, her soft fragrance enveloping him. He touched her everywhere, his expert fingers practicing their sensitive sorcery until she was moaning and arching her body against his long fingers so that he would have even more intimate access to every part of her.

He forced her hands onto his belt, forcing her to finish undoing it. Her shaking fingers clumsily slipped the leather strap through the brass buckle. He stripped out of his slacks then, out of everything, for her efforts at undressing him were too slow. Then he lifted her in his arms and carried her to the bed.

The soft mattress dipped with her slight weight. Grant followed her down, covering her pale body with his swarthy muscular one.

A shaky tremor rose helplessly in Abigail as his roving mouth plundered hers. She shouldn't let him! She shouldn't give into him, not when he was merely doing this to make their marriage legal! She forced herself to lie still and unresponsive. Perhaps if she showed no passion, he would lose interest.

His warm hands stroked the slim column of her neck, stroking downward over her golden shoulders, caressing the quickening pulsebeat at her throat. His fingers slid still farther down her creamy skin to lift the lush, ripe globes of her breasts to his hungry lips. A sudden blistering heat flamed within her as he suckled first one and then the other.

She tried to lay passive beneath him, and at last, just when she thought she could not keep from whimpering with desire, his lips ceased kissing her feverish, dampened skin.

There was no kindness in the hard black eyes that gazed harshly down at her. "It won't work, Abbie."

Her eyes widened with fear. "What?" she murmured uncomprehendingly.

"You can't play the martyred, frigid wife submitting to satisfy her husband's needs. You're too passionate for that!"

Abigail whitened. "I want to love you," she whispered, "and for you to love me."

"You don't deserve my love," he whispered. "And I don't want yours—anymore."

He lowered his lips to her soft body once more. This time when his hot tongue flicked intimately across her stiff nipple, she moaned despite her fierce determination not to. His mouth moved to the other breast.

This new, intimate exploration made Abigail's senses swirl with wondrous sensations. The pleasure was so intense that she trembled from the shock of his warm, wet mouth moving across her skin.

"Grant, no!" Abigail choked on a sob.

"You're mine, and I intend to have you," he said ruthlessly, his low voice a fierce command against her ear. She felt his warm breath stirring through her thick soft hair as she fought an inner battle for her self-control.

"No! Not like this! I can't! I won't let you!" She began to fight, but he was much stronger. Everywhere her small hands struck, they encountered unyielding muscle.

He easily shifted her body beneath the length of his own. She squirmed furiously, but her every movement merely brought a thrilling, shuddering awareness of his hardened masculinity whenever it touched her.

"Keep doing that," he whispered with a chuckle. He ran his hand down the length of her body, caressing her soft warm skin.

Defiantly she stopped, lying still at last, her soft body imprisoned beneath his. He easily molded his body to hers. The coarse black hairs of his chest scratched the tips of her breasts; his thighs melded with hers so exactly that she no longer dared to move, for her slightest movement now brought the hard insistent pressure of his love against the fluid, satiny softness of her inner thigh.

Suddenly he moved. In her panic she arched forward against him, and his flesh slid against hers so that at last it was she who allowed his body to mate deeply within hers.

Her startled blue eyes flew open, and then she snapped them shut at his broad grin and keen look of masculine triumph.

"Thank you, Abbie," he murmured with a low, warm chuckle. "I knew it would be you...who couldn't wait."

She held her eyes stubbornly closed and refused to look at him. His mouth swooped down and violently assaulted her quivering lips. She was filled with him, with the feel of his body pressing intimately into hers, with his clean male scent enveloping her. He was the world, dark and all-powerful and all-encompassing, and her whirling sensual world was him. She felt lost in the vortex of sensations he was deliberately arousing. Suddenly she knew that she had lost the will to fight, that she was scarcely a breath from yielding herself completely to him.

He began to move against her, rocking slowly, rhythmically, undulating like warm ocean waves caressing a soft shoreline, and she could resist the pressing needs of her own fevered body no longer. Her senses ruled supreme. She gloried in the pagan dance of their bodies, wrong though it was; she gloried in the erotic heat of his hands and lips exploring her womanliness, in the haze of hot, molten sensuality of a world that had gone dark and wild with primeval desires.

Grant did everything to bring her the most exquisite physical pleasure, though he did nothing to assuage the distress of her heart. And in the final blaze of their splintering passion she cried out his name and professed her love in ultimate surrender. But, though he clutched her fiercely against his hard, hot body, he said nothing of love to her.

Afterwards Abigail curled up on her own side of the lumpy bed, her passion dying away, the warmth flowing out of her. Grant kept rigidly to his own side of the bed. Her passion sated, she felt numb with emptiness as she stared in frozen pain about the depressingly impersonal room.

If only Grant had taken her to his cottage where they'd shared so many happy times instead of this place, she thought, perhaps she wouldn't feel this cold hopelessness now. Perhaps she could have more easily remembered the happier times they'd come together, both physically and lovingly. But she could scarcely recall them. They seemed a lifetime away. For the first time after he'd made love to her, she felt raw and restlessly incomplete. Without love and trust and sharing, sex couldn't bring the glow of true fulfillment, she realized miserably.

She heard the sound of his steady breathing. She longed to turn to him, to touch him, to press herself closely to him for comfort, to run her hands through his thick auburn hair. But she didn't dare. In the shadowy darkness, both his arms were crossed beneath his dark head, and he was staring up at the ceiling. She stole a glance toward his handsome face, and his grim expression only upset her all the more, for she knew he was as achingly unfulfilled as she.

Oh, what were they going to do? How were they ever going to find each other again? There seemed nothing she could say, nothing she could do to reach him. She closed her eyes and pretended to sleep, but in reality she just lay there for hours, disturbingly aware of his every restless movement until at last he roused her in the cold, black darkness and drove her back to his cottage.

The thick trees, their bare branches iced with snow, dipped low over the snow-spattered asphalt drive. The forbidding red brick mansion with its white columns loomed at the end of the black, curving ribbon. The blue Valiant whizzed bravely beneath the trees toward the deliberately pretentious Bainbridge residence. At the sight of her former home, Abigail felt the fearsome doom of a condemned prisoner en route to her execution.

She dared a nervous, sideways glance at the cold, implacably set face of her husband. It could have been a mask of bronze. He hadn't said a single word to her on the long drive to Pittsburgh. He'd scarcely spoken to her last night when they'd returned from the motel to his cottage. He'd given her his bed, while he'd slept on the couch.

When the Valiant reached the steps leading up to the front door, Grant parked directly in front of the massive oak door and switched off the motor.

"Ready?" he challenged her. His gaze raked the soft vulnerability of her face.

"I-I...this isn't going to be easy, Grant. We should have called first."

Grant laughed harshly. "And give up the dubious advantage of surprise, when it's among the few weapons I've got against Rosalind? No way!"

A convulsive shudder ran through Abigail at his angry tone. Imagining her mother's fury, she squeezed her eyelids shut for a long moment and drew a deep breath. Suddenly she felt Grant's arm circle her shoulder, and he pulled her against himself. She looked up into his face, and for an instant his harsh mask softened.

"It's going to be all right, Abbie. Trust me."

She felt his lips gently brush her forehead, and then he leaned across her soft body, the sleeve of his sheepskin coat grazing her breasts as he opened her door so that she could get out.

Frigid air gusted into the car as Abigail scrambled

out with Grant right behind her. His steadying hand was beneath her elbow, guiding her up the stairs.

The doorbell sounded ominously, and though it seemed an eternity before the door was thrust open by Williams, the pompous butler, it was in reality less than a minute.

Williams's eyes popped wide at the sight of Abigail. Then his solemn and very proper face went stern once more. "Miss Bainbridge, welcome home," he said formally.

"Mrs. Nichols," corrected Grant in a voice of steel.

Silver eyebrows lifted in the ancient face, the only sign of emotion. He eyed Grant in swift appraisal.

"Is Mrs. Bainbridge at home?" Grant demanded.

"Madame is still upstairs," Williams replied with the reserved stiffness he was famous for.

"Would you please tell her we've come to see her."

"Certainly, Mr. Nichols." Williams executed a half bow and led them across polished parquet floors beneath glittering chandeliers into the formal living room.

Abigail sank immediately onto one of the Louis XV chairs, but Grant paced as restlessly as a caged jungle beast, his eyes flicking warily to every valuable item in the room. The clicking of his boot heels upon the gleaming hardwood floors were the only sounds in the room, and they made Abigail feel even more nervous than ever.

Oh, why couldn't he be still! Why didn't he smoke or do something else that was quiet when he was nervous? At last Grant stopped, leaning toward the dark oil painting above Abigail as though to discern the artist's signature.

"The artist is Hildenbrandt, Mr. Nichols—Howard Logan Hildenbrandt," came Rosalind's carefully enunciated voice from the doorway. "He's quite renowned and the work itself is valuable, though I don't imagine that you know much about art," she added condescendingly. Grant whirled toward the sound of her voice, his handsome face dark with anger. "Hello, Abigail," Rosalind continued, ignoring him for the moment. "I wondered when you'd deem it timely to return…and face the consequences of your most disastrous behavior. I must say, you scarcely look happy."

Abigail turned absolutely white. She could think of nothing to say. It didn't seem to matter though, for Rosalind's cold attention swiftly turned back to the tall dark man beside her. Rosalind eyed him with the most witheringly disdainful look she could summon, but he met her gaze with an unwavering one of his own. At last it was she who dropped her eyes from his; pretending it was only because she couldn't resist critically examining every obnoxious detail of him.

Rosalind wanted to despise everything about him, especially the awesome maleness that his casual attire, the very sort of clothes she heartily disapproved of, enhanced. He wore jeans that molded his lean, muscular body like denim skin. Surely no decent man his age dressed as he did! His blue plaid flannel shirt stretched across his powerful shoulders, and she was unpleasantly reminded of the danger of him. He wasn't her sort at all. He didn't play by her rules, and she didn't know how to handle him. Deep within her, Rosalind knew it wasn't just his clothes and his rough background that made Grant seem so awesome, it was the man himself. And Rosalind felt shaken from the sheer force of him.

"Well, I can see I don't pass inspection," Grant began with careless indifference. "But then I hardly expected you to approve of me." A bitter edge of sarcasm laced his deep voice.

"As a matter of fact I don't, Mr. Nichols. This is the second time you've tried to ruin my daughter's life. Only this time, you may have succeeded." Rosalind glanced away from Grant, eyeing with sudden irritation his sheepskin jacket, which he'd discarded on the empty Louis XV chair beside Abigail. It was quite obviously the only item in the perfectly decorated room that did not belong. "If you wanted to

remove your jacket, Mr. Nicholas, you should have
given it to Williams, and he would have disposed
of it properly.''

Grant picked up the offending jacket and slung it
carelessly over his shoulder, the movement making
the fabric of his shirt ripple revealingly across his
muscled chest.

"Mrs. Bainbridge, as you know, I'm not used to
butlers and being waited on," he said softly.

"That's quite obvious." Again Rosalind's disdainful gaze swept from the frayed edge of his collar
down to the faded, well-washed denim length of his
powerful thighs, to the scuffed imperfection of his
boots.

"I know you're trying to make me feel that I
don't belong here with Abigail," he said.

She tilted her head back so she could look down
her long straight nose at him. "You don't."

"I don't want to belong here, Mrs. Bainbridge.
I've chosen a life that suits me much better than
living in some mausoleum like this house and amus-
ing myself by playing games with other people's
lives."

"And what, Mr. Nichols, might that be—this superior life you've chosen?"

"For your information, it's Dr. Nichols now,"
Grant said coolly.

Rosalind lifted her eyebrows in mock surprise.

There was a faint glimmer of respect in her silver eyes, though she deliberately sought to suppress it.

Grant continued, ''I want to practice medicine and do a good job of it in a small town where there aren't many doctors, where people can't always get good medical care as quickly as they need it. I don't care about money—''

''Don't you? But you've done well by yourself since we last met, haven't you? For a man who didn't have a cent to his name when we last talked, for a man who couldn't afford medical school because he had to help his family, for such a paragon who cares nothing for money. Doctors, I'm told, are scarcely a starving breed.'' There was a malicious gleam in Rosalind's eyes.

''I got through medical school, if that's what you mean. And I helped my mother, too. It wasn't easy. I had part-time jobs because I had to help my mother and sisters. Somehow my mother was able to get a loan. I've worked in Africa for three years at a Third World hospital in the jungle.''

''How very noble and self-sacrificing.'' Rosalind's voice was acidic.

''Not really. It was simply what I wanted to do.''

''I find that terribly easy to believe, Dr. Nichols. I'm sure you were much more at ease in the jungle than you could ever be in civilized surroundings.'' Rosalind paused to let her barb settle. ''I'm sure, however, that you did not come here today to discuss your medical career. Tell me, why did you come? What do you want now? Is it money—again?''

The line of Grant's mouth was tight and grim. A nerve spasmed along the edge of his jaw.

''I never wanted money from you! And you know it! But I did come here today because you have something I want.''

''I never doubted it. Your own personal gain has always been your only interest in my daughter!''

Grant took a step toward the older woman, and there was danger in his dark face. He forced himself to stop even as she backed fearfully away. Anger blazed from the deep blackness of his eyes. In the moment of absolute silence that followed her remark, not even Rosalind dared to speak.

Was her mother right? Was Grant's only interest in her his own personal gain? A terrible coldness swept through Abigail, a coldness that reached right down to the center of her soul. If only...if only Grant would deny what her mother said. But he did not. He did nothing but stare at her mother.

''I came for Michael, my son,'' Grant managed at last in a hard, clipped voice. ''That's all I want from you, Mrs. Bainbridge!''

''And the only reason you want him is because you know I'll pay to keep him.''

Grant was terribly still, and Abigail was afraid—of Grant and what he might do if her mother continued to push him. Abigail sprang from her chair and stepped between these two warring people she loved. Their hatred and anger were tearing her apart.

"Mother," Abigail began gently, "don't say things like that to Grant. They're not true! You don't know Grant like I do. He's not what you think. He's not the man I believed he was—the man you told me he was. I've seen him working with little children and caring for elderly sick people. Everybody in the village idolizes him, because they recognize what kind of man he is. He gives of himself because he genuinely cares about suffering people, because he wants to help them, whether he gets paid or not!"

Her mother stared at her with a terrible, forbidding fury. And because Abigail was looking at her mother, she failed to note the swift blaze of conflicting emotions that played across Grant's dark face at her defense of him—surprise, joy, forgiveness, love—before it went blank once more.

Suddenly Abigail wondered if her mother would ever understand. Was her world too narrow for her to tolerate another's viewpoint? With a tiny sob, Abigail flung herself into Grant's arms, not knowing if he would reject her or not. When she felt his strong arms circle her body with a fierce possessiveness, she sank against him in relief. She felt his warm lips in her hair as he pressed her close as though she were very dear to him.

"I will never give either of you Michael!" Rosalind said coldly.

"You won't have a choice," Grant said in a hard voice that was equally cold. "Where is he, Mrs. Bainbridge?"

Rosalind stared back at them both furiously. "He's not here! I've sent him away—to school."

Abigail felt the tightening of Grant's grip at her waist. "Oh, Mother, no... No! You can't do that! Not to Michael!"

"As his legal guardian, I can do what I deem suitable and best for him. It's a very fine school, I can assure you. Very expensive."

"I know all about fine, expensive schools, Mother," Abigail cried.

"Perhaps you were not sent away early enough, Abigail darling. I don't intend to make the same mistake with Michael that I made with you."

"Mother, you're only doing this to Michael to punish me. Please—"

Grant's voice cut in. "Mrs. Bainbridge, you are no longer within your legal rights where Michael is concerned. I'm warning you that if you don't do as I wish in this matter and let me have my son, in the very near future you will lose both Abigail and Michael. Grandparents don't have as many rights with respect to grandchildren as you seem to think.''

Rosalind continued to stand ramrod straight, but she'd gone pale beneath the perfection of her makeup. ''Rights,'' she whispered in a voice that had gone hoarse, so intense was her emotion. ''Who are you to speak to me about rights to Michael? Though you call him your son, you have no right to him. For eight years you did nothing for him. I've supported him, paid for him. I'm his legal guardian.''

''Not anymore!'' Grant inserted. ''Abigail is my wife now, and when she married me, she became his legal guardian. And as for the past eight years, I didn't know I had a son, because neither of you told me! But now that I do, I'll reimburse you every penny you or anybody else spent in his support. I never had a chance to do anything for him before!''

''And what could you have done for him? Eight years ago you had nothing to give either my daughter or a son except a life of squalid poverty. Your mother was in need of an expensive operation that you couldn't give her.'' Rosalind paused. ''And you wouldn't have anything right now it it weren't for me. The money that paid for your mother's operation and the cost of your medical education came from this check I gave you and your family to stay away from Abigail.'' With that Rosalind pulled a crumpled cancelled check from her pocket and thrust it into Abigail's shaking fingers. "As far as I'm concerned, I've been more than generous to you!"

Abigail scarcely had a chance to read the name Nichols and the amount of $10,000, before Grant ripped the paper from her fingertips and read it for himself. He flipped the check over and read the endorsement. A look of dark puzzlement etched his hard features.

"Grant," Abigail implored. "Please tell me it isn't so, that you didn't take money...as a bribe to stay away from me." His dark, handsome face swam in the blur of her tears.

"Abbie, if you even have to ask, then there's no hope for us," Grant muttered angrily. "Mrs. Bainbridge, don't think for a minute you've heard the last of me."

Abigail buried her face in her hands. She heard the furious clatter of his boots grow dim as they echoed like hollow sounds down the hallway. When she looked up he was gone, and she was alone with Rosalind. Rosalind was smiling faintly, triumphantly, and yet there was bitter pain in her smile.

It flitted through Abigail's mind that money was a horrible responsibility. It shouldn't be used to buy and sell people, to manipulate people. If Grant had taken the money, he had done so because he desperately needed it, and Rosalind had played upon that need.

Suddenly Abigail knew that no matter what he'd done, she had to go after him. In time she would forgive him, because she loved him too much to live without him.

"Grant!" It was a soul-wrenching cry that only caused him to quicken his steps.

He stormed out of the house like an angry giant. The front door opened and slammed as though blown shut with the force of a tornado.

Tears streamed down her face as Abigail ran after him "Grant, come back!"

But when she opened the door and the frozen air swept into the house, swirling her skirt about her knees, she saw with horror that he'd left without her. The blue Valiant was speeding up the drive, vanishing beneath the shadows cast by the trees.

"Grant..." His name was a whisper blown away with the wind.

He was gone, and she felt that he was lost to her forever!

Twelve

"**W**hat really happened, Mother?"

The simple question cracked like a whip in the silent grandeur of Rosalind's living room. Startled, Rosalind's silver head pivoted toward the slim, poised figure at the doorway who held herself erectly as though what she was doing was terribly difficult for her. A quiver of inexplicable fear traced through Rosalind, yet at the same moment she felt both sympathy and pride as she looked at her daughter. For the first time Abigail was, in reality, the polished, mature young woman she'd pretended to be for so many years.

"What do you mean?" Rosalind asked coolly.

"I mean that if you and I are going to have a relationship from this point forth, you'd better tell me the whole truth about what happened eight years ago."

The steady blue eyes that met her mother's lacked their familiar, childish vulnerability, and Rosalind felt that terrible sense of loss all mothers feel the moment it comes to them that their child is no longer a child. She didn't know quite what to do. She only knew she felt extremely uncomfortable with this challenging young woman who stood before her.

"You would choose him over me—over your family?" Rosalind asked, her question a bewildered accusation deliberately phrased to make Abigail cringe with guilt for this betrayal.

Abigail nodded gently, still with that same shining determination and without a trace of the guilt that Rosalind had hoped to arouse. "I don't want to, Mother," she began softly, "but I love Grant too much to give him up. I'm going after him right now if you don't tell me, and I don't intend to come back—except to get Michael. Maybe Grant won't have me, but I have to fight for him. I'm through letting you or anyone else run my life. I may have made some mistakes, but I've sure paid for them. And what you did—trying to whitewash everything and pretend it never happened—only made everything worse. I don't think I really grew up until

Grant walked out of this house a minute ago, and I knew that if I was going to make any sense of myself as a human being, I had to start living my own life. I'm me! Not you! I don't care about five generations of Bainbridges!

"I know you think Grant's all wrong for me, but he's a fine man. And he loves me, even though I've hurt him terribly—I know he does! And I love him! I know we can make it, if we just have half a chance. Mother, you can't think for me, you can't love for me and you can't tell me how to live anymore. I'm a mother, too, but for eight years I've had to pretend I wasn't because it wouldn't look right to people. Well, I'm through pretending. I'm through with a lot of things. I'm through with dot pictures and forks and—"

"Forks?" Even in her distress at this passionate and disturbing declaration, Rosalind couldn't make sense out of where forks fit in.

Abigail smiled faintly in understanding. "Never mind. Just tell me what happened eight years ago. Did you lie to me about Grant?"

Rosalind's bleak silver gaze met her daughter's, and she saw determination and strength that more than matched her own. Despite the depressing turn of events and her uneasiness and fear for the future, Rosalind's expression held the faintest beginnings of admiration and respect.

"Abigail, whatever I've done, I've always loved you," she said weakly.

"I know that, Mother."

"I thought what I was doing was for the best, that he was just some crazy puppy love you'd get out of your system. And at first I thought he was just a fast one on the make. You were so young, and he seemed so wrong. But as I got to know him, I realized he wasn't what I thought he was at all, though I'd never met anyone quite so passionate and so obstinate as he was. He was very difficult to deal with, let me assure you. He was poor, but so terribly angry and proud. I knew he'd never let me help you and make things easier for you if he married you. He wouldn't have taken a penny. He would have struggled so, and you were so spoiled, I just didn't think...I couldn't imagine you living like that. I didn't want to see you marry the wrong man and grow disillusioned with all the responsibilities and hardships of such a marriage. You were just a child."

Abigail sighed with mature understanding instead of anger. "Maybe you were right," she said wearily. "I just let you take over and make all the decisions, which I meekly accepted. If I'd been an adult, I wouldn't have done that. Maybe I couldn't have handled those things." She paused. "What about that check Grant has that you said was a bribe?"

Rosalind brightened with shame. "It wasn't a bribe," she admitted. "He didn't know a thing about it until today."

"Then…"

"Well, he was such a stubbornly forceful young man, and though I thought he was all wrong for you, I could see he had some rather admirable qualities when he wasn't letting his pride get in the way. I did some checking into his background and discovered that his grades in medical school were quite spectacular and that his professors thought he was gifted as well with the compassionate kind of nature that makes for a truly wonderful doctor. I thought of all the impersonal charities I gave money to, and finally I summoned the courage to go to his mother. Grant was, after all, the father of my expected grandchild. Mrs. Nichols was quite ill, and well, darling, I'm afraid I appealed to her maternal pride to make her accept the money as a loan. Grant was quite determined to quit school and see after her."

"And so, because of you, Grant is a doctor."

Abigail came to her mother and circled her shoulders with her arms. They held each other for a long silent time.

"I wouldn't say that, darling. I helped him. That's all. He's much too stubborn and hard-headed to have given up."

"So he did come after me…" Abigail said wist-

fully, thinking sadly of all the years she'd tried to
hate him because she believed he hadn't.

"Oh, yes, many many times. The first time he
stormed in here, you were still in Pittsburgh and out
with your father. I was dreadfully frightened you
would come home before I could get rid of him.
That's when I decided I had to send you away."

"But where was he that night we left Aunt
Peggy's and went to his cottage and all his clothes
were gone?"

Rosalind's gaze wavered, and she felt a piercing
pang of guilt. "His mother was terribly ill and in
the hospital, darling, and he'd gone to her. He left
a letter for you explaining everything, in the kitchen
of that dreary little cottage. Do you remember how
I went in the house first? I got the letter myself and
destroyed it."

"Oh, Mother…"

"I'm not proud of what I did, but I can't say I'm
thrilled you married him instead of Harold. But go
to him, darling, if you love him so. And I'll tell you
where Michael is, so you two can go after him when
you've made up. Michael will be wild with joy
when he sees you, because I'm afraid he didn't want
to go away to school at all. You can borrow my car
if you need it."

"Thank you, Mother."

"I suppose Grant is terribly good-looking in a rugged sort of way," Rosalind admitted at last. "And you know, I think Michael's every bit as stubborn as he is. I'm not sure Grant will be all that easy to live with, Abigail."

"Mother—" Abigail smiled fondly down at Rosalind "—I'm used to strong personalities."

Abigail drove slowly, the murmur of her mother's white Mercedes like the purr of a great white cat creeping through the slick, narrow streets. The houses sat right on the snow-covered road, looking like squashed cereal boxes with gabled roofs that had been stacked one right after the other in scrunched rows. There was no room between them, and they scarcely had front yards. Behind these houses belched the furnaces of the steel mills. A train whistled shrilly nearby, and even in the muted interior of the Mercedes, Abigail could hear the seemingly ceaseless rumble of freight cars on the nearby railroad track.

Abigail didn't know this part of Pittsburgh, and from time to time she had to pull over to the side of the road to study her city map. Suddenly she saw what she was looking for; the tip of her toe touched the accelerator in excitement and trepidation.

Her heart leaped with joy and then beat faster

with fear at the sight of Grant's blue Valiant parked in the gravel drive beside one of the squat houses.

Abigail parked the car in front of the narrow little house and stepped out into the snow. She walked up the drive, careful of the unshoveled snow and ice. Here there were no servants to keep the yards and drives. She knocked hesitantly on the door and waited in fearful suspense.

At last the front door opened, though the storm door remained closed. Grant glared coldly at her through the glass before he pushed it open for her. She stepped into the small living room without being invited in.

Nervously she looked away from his glittering harsh eyes. She heard the exuberant scoldings of an older woman's voice in a tiny den on the other side of the kitchen, as well as the vibrant shouts of what sounded like an army of small children. There was the scent and sizzle of chicken frying and mashed potatoes steaming.

The environment of the small house was warmly cozy, the place inviting for all its plainness. It was obvious to Abigail the minute she stepped inside that the house was not just a house, but the most cheerful of homes. So this was where Grant had grown up.

"Allow me to play butler," Grant jeered, forcing her attention back to himself. His strong warm hands brushed her shoulders as he took her coat, their touch burning her through her thin dress.

Her chin lifted instinctively with hurt. "Grant, don't...please. You don't know...how ashamed I feel," she pleaded.

"To be here amidst—how did your mother put it—such squalid poverty?"

"No, of course not. I'm ashamed...of myself."

He gazed ruthlessly down at her. Her beautiful face was so pale, her eyes brilliant with fierce pain. He fought against the softening in his heart.

"You had no business coming here," he said, but his tone had gentled ever so slightly.

"Grant, don't shut me out of your life, please," she whispered softly. "I can't live without you."

He jammed his balled fists into the pockets of his jeans and said shortly, "You lived without me happily enough for eight damn years and caught yourself a millionaire in the bargain. Maybe your mother was right when she said I've never had anything I could give either you or my son."

"You don't believe that."

"This isn't exactly what you're accustomed to."

"Grant, you can't believe all the things my mother said."

"No, but sometimes I can't help wondering if you do."

"I don't, and for your information, I doubt if she

does either. My mother will say absolutely anything in the heat of an argument if she thinks it will help her win it. She doesn't care whom she hurts, but when she's in a different mood, she can be a very caring person. She's really very sorry about everything."

There was a noise in the kitchen, and a large woman with a cheerful face beneath short-cropped salt-and-pepper hair stepped into the living room.

"Hello there." She spoke in a friendly manner that disarmed some of the explosive tension between Abigail and Grant. She was carrying a measuring cup she'd obviously been dipping in flour.

"You're Grant's mother." Abigail's voice was gentle with awe as the older woman took her hand in hers. "And I-I'm Abigail."

"Yes of course. I know all about you—from Grant as well as your mother. I've seen your picture in all the papers. Even since I met your mother eight years ago, I've kept up with you in the society pages." Mrs. Nichols's black eyes snapped with enthusiasm. She obviously had a strong, irrepressible personality. "I'm so glad Grant married you."

Abigail felt herself warming toward the older woman. "You met my mother..."

"Yes, dear. Grant and I..." She cast Grant a dubious, motherly glance. "Well, I'm afraid we've been having words...over that check he brought here from your mother. It's all my fault, dear, what's gone wrong between you," she plunged in despite Grant's warning look. "You see, it was I, and not Grant, who borrowed the money from your mother. He didn't know a thing about it. You see, I knew he was too proud to take a penny. But I was so sick at the time, and I couldn't help him with his school. The girls weren't on their own, and my husband had just died. Your mother explained to me how she had so much money that she would never miss it, that we could take as long as we wanted to repay it, that she wanted her money to do something really useful. She came to this house several times. And we had long talks about both you and Grant. She explained how you were too young for marriage, and I knew what getting through medical school meant to Grant. She seemed so genuinely interested in helping Grant. When she said he was ambitious and de-served a chance, I completely agreed with her. I never thought I was doing anything wrong by taking the money, don't you see? I thought I was simply a mother doing what was best for my son."

The constriction in Abigail's throat made it im-possible for her to speak for a minute, but she moved toward the older woman, took her hand in her own and squeezed it tightly. At last in a choked voice she said, "You didn't do anything wrong."

"It seems," Grant said with the faintest hint of a

smile, "that rich, influential mothers are not the only meddlers in their children's lives."

"Yes," Mrs. Nichols murmured in a low, ashamed voice. "Grant, I wouldn't have hurt you for the world. I wouldn't have taken the money if I'd known it would cause these problems for you and your wife."

"I know, Mother."

"And, son, you worked so hard to repay every penny of that loan plus a generous amount of interest. It wasn't as if you took anything without paying for it."

"I see you've got this very well rationalized," he said with tender indulgence. "But, no...I don't suppose it was like taking something gratis." Grant turned toward Abigail, and the intensity of his gaze left her breathless. "Someday soon I'm going to have to thank your mother, Abbie, for helping my family the way she did. In spite of her personal feelings toward me, she gave me a chance to realize a lifelong dream, and she helped my mother back to robust health."

Mrs. Nichols wisely tripped out of the room on the pretense that she needed to monitor the children she was baby-sitting and see after the meal she was cooking.

"Your mother's a wonderful lady, Grant," Abigail said in admiration.

"Abigail…" Grant's low voice was soft, pregnant with passion and love.

The smile that flitted across her lips was tremulous; her blue eyes gleamed with her love.

"I love you, Abbie. I can't seem to stop even when I want to."

A wild song was singing in her veins as she looked up at him in sudden shyness. "How well I know that feeling," she murmured.

They were in each other's arms.

His hands were smoothing the tumbling masses of her hair from her face so that he could kiss her with hungry lips, possessing hers with the insatiable need of a man who'd longed for this moment more than anything on earth.

"I was poor, Abbie, but never deprived. I had the love and support of a wonderful family. Sure, things were tough sometimes, and sometimes we had to do without. But I'm not sure it ever hurt any of us. I don't love you for your money, Abbie, and no amount would be large enough to bribe me to leave you—not in the past and not in the future. I want you to believe that. It's you I want. Simply you."

"I know that. I should have always known that."

"You were young," he excused her, and then he kissed her wildly with such torrid intensity she was shaking. "And I was a fool."

"And I didn't trust you enough," she whispered

against the hot urgency of his mouth, "or I would never have believed you capable of the things I did."

"I believed your mother, too," he muttered.

"She was," Abigail said sadly, "only doing what she believed was best, and today she gave me the address of Michael's school. Maybe someday you'll be able to forgive her."

"Maybe someday…when we have Michael and a life of our own that she's given up trying to disrupt. But right now, I want to concentrate on loving you. Tomorrow will be soon enough to worry about Michael and your mother."

His arms were around her in a fiercely intimate embrace. Her dark lashes fluttered downward in response to his passion. He kissed her so passionately again that they were each aware only of the wonder of the other and the roaring love that consumed them.

Epilogue

"When your mother sends a kid away, she sure sends him the hell away!" Grant said shortly, drawing a swift sharp breath as he glanced toward the academy's school buildings. "This place certainly wasn't easy to get to—two layovers and a rental car." Clutching Abigail's hand in his, he deliberately stepped nearer the edge of the hill they had climbed, pulling her with him so they could look out at the view. In the brilliant sunshine the town with its trees and river and private school was spread before them. "Texas! I never even heard of this town 'til now."

"That must be the courthouse over there," Abigail said, pointing to a prominent building in the center of the town square. "And that must be the amusement park we read about. Maybe if we have enough time, we can take Michael there before we have to drive back to Austin and catch our plane...."

Abigail chattered brightly as if she had to keep talking to cover the awkwardness that she was so keenly aware Grant was feeling.

Suddenly Grant's grip tightened around her slender fingers, and his arm moved about her shoulders. She looked up at him and saw the leaping light in his black eyes as they followed the meandering path of a solitary figure high above them upon the brown hillside. An eager little boy with wavy auburn hair and a suntanned face yelped suddenly at the sight of them.

"Aunt Abigail!"

Abigail heard the cry as Michael sprinted enthusiastically toward them. Grant took a step forward and then stopped.

"Abbie, I don't know what I'm going to say to him."

"You'll know, darling," she said reassuringly. "But you don't even have to say anything if you can't."

Grant devoured every feature of his little boy as the child raced headlong down the hill and flung himself into Abigail's outstretched arms.

"Did you come to take me home?" Michael asked breathlessly, pulling away from her smothering kisses.

"Yes, dearest. Oh, yes." Abigail hugged him fiercely and looked up into Grant's proud gaze.

Grant knelt down beside them, and Michael's gaze met and held the grave black eyes that were the exact shade of his own.

"Michael, dearest, this is Grant Nichols, my husband," she said softly, hating that she couldn't tell him the whole truth until he was old enough to understand.

"He's the man that stole you in the church and made Grandmother so mad!" Michael blurted in excitement and awe.

Michael studied the big dark stranger with great interest, scarcely listening to his aunt's jumbled response.

"You're going to live with us now, Michael," Abigail explained gently, stroking his dark head affectionately. "Would you like that?"

"Yes."

Abigail was terribly aware of Grant's aching silence, and her heart went out to him.

"And this afternoon Grant and I wanted to do something special before we catch our plane—something that you would really enjoy, just to celebrate the beginning of our lives together. Would you like to go down to the amusement park on the river? Or is there something else you would rather do?''

''Well, really I'd rather...go to a movie, Aunt Abigail. *E.T.* is showing downtown. I saw the commercial for it on TV.''

''But you've already seen it several times, Michael,'' Abigail protested, without looking at Grant.

''I like going to movies about better than anything. And good movies get better every time you see them,'' Michael said sagely. ''Do you know what I mean?''

Abigail merely stared at the diminutive replica of the man she loved. Unlike Grant she never liked to watch a movie more than once.

Suddenly Grant was chuckling, his barrier of silence broken, and the deep warm sound enveloped all three of them. ''Yes, son, I know what you mean. Old movies just keep getting better and better the more times you see them, don't they?''

Above Michael's head, Grant's eyes met Abigail's shining gaze, and she knew this moment was their beginning.

*   *   *   *   *

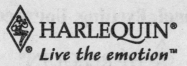

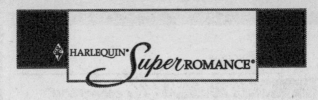

HARLEQUIN® *Super*ROMANCE®

...there's more to the story!

Superromance.
A *big* satisfying read about unforgettable
characters. Each month we offer *six* very different
stories that range from family drama to adventure
and mystery, from highly emotional stories to
romantic comedies—and much more! Stories
about people you'll believe in and care about.
Stories too compelling to put down....

Our authors are among today's *best* romance
writers. You'll find familiar names and talented
newcomers. Many of them are award winners—
and you'll see why!

If you want the biggest and best
in romance fiction, you'll get it
from Superromance!

Emotional, Exciting, Unexpected...

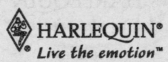

HARLEQUIN®
Live the emotion™

Harlequin Historicals®
Historical Romantic Adventure!

From rugged lawmen and valiant knights to defiant heiresses and spirited frontierswomen, Harlequin Historicals will capture your imagination with their dramatic scope, passion and adventure.

Harlequin Historicals . . . they're too good to miss!

HHDIR104

HARLEQUIN®
INTRIGUE®

WE'LL LEAVE YOU BREATHLESS!

If you've been looking for thrilling tales of
contemporary passion and sensuous love stories
with taut, edge-of-the-seat suspense—then
you'll love Harlequin Intrigue!

Every month, you'll meet six new heroes
who are guaranteed to make your spine tingle
and your pulse pound. With them you'll enter
into the exciting world of Harlequin Intrigue—
where your life is on the line
and so is your heart!

THAT'S INTRIGUE—
ROMANTIC SUSPENSE
AT ITS BEST!

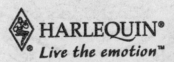

HARLEQUIN®
Live the emotion™